UNWRAPPED
A SECOND CHANCE, CHRISTMAS ROMANCE

SUGAR & SPICE
BOOK ONE

ALEXIS WINTER

SUGAR & SPICE

With flirty encounters, heated chocolate moments, and holiday magic woven throughout, **Unwrapped** delivers the perfect blend of sugar, spice, and everything nice. I promise!

SUGAR & SPICE

WHEN MY BEST FRIEND AND I DECIDE TO OPEN OUR DREAM BAKERY, SUGAR & SPICE, I EXPECT ENDLESS NIGHTS OF KNEADING DOUGH AND DUSTING SUGAR COOKIES WITH HOLIDAY MAGIC.

What I don't expect?

My business-savvy bestie reaching out to Asher Mercer—Chicago's most eligible bachelor and the same guy who starred in all my high school daydreams.

He's everything I remember—devastatingly handsome, wickedly charming—with a gaze that makes my knees weak and my pulse race faster than an industrial mixer.

I'm not that quiet girl hiding behind textbooks anymore, but sitting across from him in a high-stakes business meeting, watching him study my proposal like he's savoring the last bite of dessert, has my composure threatening to crack.

Between building our business and perfecting every recipe these last few years, I've convinced myself that love is just another ingredient I don't have time to measure.

But when Asher starts showing up more often with questions about dreams that have nothing to do with profit margins, I feel my carefully constructed walls beginning to crumble like an overbaked cookie.

One kiss beneath the mistletoe at his company's holiday party changes everything.

Now, with success finally within reach, I'm faced with an impossible choice: stick to my tried-and-true recipe for success, or risk it all on a taste of something sweeter.

After all, some of the best desserts require turning up the heat.

THANK YOU!

A heartfelt thank you to my amazing readers for continuing to support my dream of bringing sexy, naughty, delicious little morsels of fun in the form of romance novels.

A special thank you to my incredible editor, Kimberly Stripling, without whom I would be completely lost!

Thank you to my fantastic cover designer, Sarah Kil, who always brings my visions to life in the most outstanding ways.

And lastly, to my ARC team and beta readers—you are wonderful, and I couldn't do this without you.

xoxo,
Alexis Winter

CHAPTER 1
IVY

"Oh, the weather outside is—hmm, hmm, hmm."

I hum along blissfully to the familiar Christmas tune as I whisk together a blend of spices for our latest batch of holiday cookies—vanilla chai pecan tassies. The scent of cinnamon and nutmeg fills my tiny Chicago apartment, wrapping around me like a warm hug. Not only is it my favorite time of year but it's also the last time I'll be doing this in my apartment.

It's a tradition I started almost a decade ago when I was just trying to make a few extra bucks in college. Back then, I could barely keep up with the demand of making a few batches for Christmas or big game days on campus. But once the frat boys found out I made cookies and spread the word to their stoner friends, the orders rolled in, and I knew I needed help.

That's when Tessa came in. My best friend, my partner in crime, and my opposite in nearly every way. She's sprawled across my worn-out couch now, legs tucked beneath her, her perfectly golden hair pulled back in a messy bun that somehow manages to look chic.

The laughter comes easily between us, just like it always has. But when we were younger, it was boys and high school drama that

1

captivated our attention. Now it's business decisions and avoiding the fact that we are both pushing thirty and still single... something I think we both hope to change.

"Can you believe we're actually doing this?" Tessa's voice cuts through my thoughts, her excitement barely contained as she twists a peppermint candy between her fingers. "Opening Sugar & Spice, our dream bakery?" Her mouth hangs open, her eyes about to bulge out of her head like she's just having the thought for the first time.

"Yes." I smile, but then just as quickly it disappears. "And no," I confess, my chest tightening with nerves.

"What? Why?" She pouts, her excitement deflating just as quickly as her smile.

This tradition of ours—baking holiday treats in my little apartment—has always been the highlight of my year. Hanging out with my best friend while we dance around to holiday hits and dream of the future. But now, all those dreams are becoming reality. This isn't just a fun way to make some extra cash. We're quitting our big girl jobs and sinking every last dime we have into this.

This year, it's not just for fun—it's for our dream.

"I'm excited, I promise." I try to sound convincing. "It's surreal, after all those years of talking about it, but um, yeah." I swallow down the nerves. "It's finally happening. I just hope the bank sees it that way, too. I, uh, got a little nervous when the lender kept calling, asking for so many last-minute documents I thought we'd already sent over."

Tessa rolls her eyes. "They will; they already have. They're just doing their due diligence, and with how many people touch the lending process, it's bound to have some hiccups. Besides." She smiles broadly. "How could they resist? Our business plan is flawless. Well, mostly because I wrote it." She flips her hair over her shoulder, a playful smirk on her lips. "I'm Boss Barbie, remember? Should I pull that Halloween costume out of hiding and wear it to our final loan meeting? I think Todd might like it."

"Todd would have a heart attack." I laugh, an image of our sixty-eight-year-old loan manager clutching his chest if he saw Tess walk in with her tits up to her chin. I throw a dishtowel at her, and she catches it, laughing.

"I'm kidding, but seriously, our plan is solid. Plus, we've both lived in shoeboxes and saved every spare penny for the last seven years to make this happen. We've got this, babe."

Tessa's confidence is something I envy. Even though she's been my best friend since we were seven, it never quite rubbed off on me. While she's the one who can charm a room with just her smile, I've always been the quiet one, preferring the comfort of books and recipes to networking events.

She was the one who marched over to my front yard when she saw us moving in and said, *"Hey, I'm Tessa,"* with her hand outstretched and a smile plastered across her face. *"I'm seven, and I live over there. I have two cats—do you like cats?"*

We've been inseparable ever since. Even through high school, when she was the head cheerleader, prom queen, and student body president, while I was—invisible. Not that I minded it. I never felt the need to try and blend in with her popular friends, and she never once excluded me from anything.

I was happy to hang back at home on weekends when she'd invite me to a party at one of the football players' houses or another cheerleader's sleepover—until Asher Mercer joined the team, and I fell head over heels for a guy who probably wouldn't have said a word to me if I hadn't been Tessa's shadow.

The Mercer brothers were well-known even back then—practically small-town royalty.

Asher was the golden boy, the quarterback with a dazzling smile who seemed to glide through life with everything falling perfectly into place. And Zane, his older brother, was the opposite—brooding, mysterious, always on the outskirts of the social scene.

If Asher was the sun, Zane was the dark, uncharted side of the moon. He got into trouble, skipped classes, and even managed to get kicked out of college. Rumor had it he ran some kind of resale business out of his parents' garage in high school, making bank basically helping businesses find tax breaks and whatnot but no one really knew what he was up to.

They were like us in a way. Tessa, the ever exuberant and outgoing center of attention, and me. While I wasn't the brooding troublemaker Zane might have been, we were both the outsiders. The weird kids at school who kept to ourselves and had maybe one real friend who understood us. Although with Zane, I'm not sure he had anyone besides Asher who understood him. And if memory serves me right, it wasn't just the school and local authorities that felt Zane was a screwup; his dad fired him from working at their family insurance company when he was only sixteen.

I remember watching Asher from a distance, how he'd joke with his friends and turn the whole school into his audience. But he wasn't just popular; he was kind, even if he didn't realize it at the time.

Once, when Tessa dragged me to a bonfire party after a football game, I spilled my drink all over myself and wanted to disappear. Asher had handed me a towel, smiling in that easy way of his. "*Happens to the best of us,*" he'd said with a lopsided smile, and for a second, I thought I might melt right into the ground.

My hand actually shook when I reached out to grab the towel from him. And in that brief second, the way his eyes met mine, I felt seen and even though I was covered in sweet, sticky who knows what—for once, I didn't want the ground to open up and swallow me.

Tessa had teased me about it for weeks after it happened, and I'd blushed every time his name came up. I convinced myself that it was just a silly crush—nothing more than admiration from afar. But there were moments when I'd catch Asher looking my way, and I'd wonder if maybe he saw me as more than just Tessa's quiet friend.

But that delusion quickly vanished when I'd see his arm wrapped around Josie Callaghan's teeny tiny waist, a flirtatious giggle tumbling from her perfect bubblegum lips whenever he leaned in to whisper something to her.

"You're right," I say more confidently, bringing myself back to the present, "and we really do make some damn good cookies." I take a bite from a warm double chocolate peppermint cookie I've just pulled from the oven and close my eyes, a soft sigh slipping past my lips.

"You make a damn good cookie." Tessa laughs. "I'm just the business bitch." I'm only half listening, my eyes still closed as I savor the final crumbs of the cookie.

"You sure you don't need a moment alone with that?" she asks, laughter in her voice.

"I was having one, but you ruined it," I say, rubbing my hands against my apron. "You know I like to savor the first test bite of every batch—it's how I can tell if any of the ratios are off."

"So scientific," Tessa mocks playfully.

"I am, in fact, a scientist," I remind her, "and baking is chemistry."

"For now," she says, her tone turning more serious. "Soon, your only titles will finally be baker and business owner." She smiles.

"Crazy to think, huh?"

I glance around my kitchen, the same one we've been baking out of for the last five years while I worked in research and Tessa jumped from one marketing job to another, continuing to climb the ladder but always with our bakery dream in mind. That pang of nostalgia tightens my throat, making it grow thick with emotion.

"Hey," Tessa says, her voice softer as if she's trying to pull me out of my own head. "Remember that time." She starts to laugh. "That time that you mel—" Her laughter keeps interrupting her. "Melted the spatula to the cookie sheet because—" She's laughing so hard she can't get through the story, and it's starting to spread to me.

"It was three a.m.!" I say through tears as we both relive the memory of staying up until the most unholy of hours to get a few more final batches of cookies done for the holidays. We learned the hard way that year that you cannot, in fact, design, bake, cool, decorate, and package fifty dozen cookies in a weekend with only two people—unless you want to end up so sleep-deprived you almost burn your apartment building down.

"Oh God." I clutch my stomach, a cramp starting to form from laughing so hard. "And we can't forget that one and only time we rented a commercial kitchen place and somehow managed to mangle the mixer arm."

I cringe at the memory of the $600 mistake that night cost us. Yet another sobering reality that we can't afford to be making those kinds of mistakes anymore, not with so much riding on our back.

"You know what I love thinking about?" She pushes away from the couch, walking over to the island. "Watching everyone's reaction the first time they bite into one of your cookies." She grabs a spatula and begins to remove the fresh cookies, placing them onto cooling racks. "Not just because they're delicious, always with the perfect amount of softness to the inside, but because you put your heart and soul into each recipe and it shows."

The silence hangs between us for a moment, a tear teetering on the rim of my eye.

"Thank you." I laugh through the sentiment, shaking my head and wiping away the tear that eventually tumbles down my cheek. "I don't know why I'm crying over it."

"Because this is huge; we're about to change our lives."

We reminisce even more about the nights in our tiny, cramped studio apartment after college. How a huge weekend for us that first year was making enough money to buy beer and a bottle of vodka if we were lucky.

But eventually, the conversation drifts to the familiar, a topic I've tried to avoid for years—men, or more specifically, the lack of them in our lives.

Tessa tosses her oven mitts onto the counter, crossing her arms over her chest and leaning her hip against the counter.

"Ivy, we need dates. I'm serious. We're like two steps away from adopting cats and talking to them about our feelings."

I snort. "There's nothing wrong with cats. You love cats. You had a cat until last year, actually. Rest in peace, Meatball," I say softly. Tessa smiles at the mention of her eighteen-year-old cat—a tender topic to this date.

"Yeah, but there's something wrong with spending another holiday season alone, right?"

I shrug, focusing on the dough in front of me. "Hardly seems like the time to jump into trying to find a relationship when we're opening a business."

The truth is, I've never really had the patience for dating, and the idea of putting myself out there is terrifying. Besides, I've always convinced myself that guys like Asher Mercer—the smooth-talking, always-smiling CEO of Mercer Enterprises, the center of my secret little high school crush I've continued to harbor—don't go for girls like me.

"I'm not saying we need to find Prince Charming by New Year's, just a guy who doesn't make you want to crawl out of your skin or gnaw your own arm off trying to get out of the date."

"Wow," I say dryly, "the bar is literally in hell."

"I'm just saying we deserve to have some fun is all. We've been busting our asses for years and it wouldn't kill either of us to get laid more than twice a year."

"I can agree to that." I knead the dough a little harder, my tension ratcheted up to eleven.

Tessa suddenly perks up, her eyes sparkling with mischief. "Speaking of dates, I bet you haven't forgotten about Asher Mercer."

I freeze, my cheeks burning as I try to keep my expression neutral. "What? Why would I remember him?"

"Because you had the biggest crush on him in high school," she teases, leaning forward. "Don't even try to deny it, Ivy. You used to turn into a blushing mess whenever he was around."

I roll my eyes. "That was years ago, Tess. And it wasn't *whenever he was around*. It was one time that I got a little— And besides, he's not exactly my type." I focus my attention on rolling out the dough to the perfect thickness, then I grab my holiday cookie cutters and stamp out a dozen shapes.

"I too hate it when my crush is a six-three blue-eyed god that could make angels weep with his jawline."

I roll my eyes, placing the cutouts onto the cookie sheet. "I'm just saying he's very famous, out there on social media and celebrity events. He's an extrovert to the fullest."

"Sure, whatever you say," she singsongs, but there's a knowing smile on her face. "It's just funny because I happened to connect with him on LinkedIn recently. And I was thinking... since we're about to open a business, why not get some advice from a local expert?"

I nearly drop the cookie sheet. "What? No. Absolutely not."

"Oh, come on! They run one of the fastest-growing companies in the Midwest according to *Forbes*. Plus, they're both on the 30 Under 30 list of richest US bachelors. They could look over our business plan before we make an offer on that building."

I pause, considering it. As much as the idea of seeing Asher again sends my nerves into overdrive, Tessa isn't wrong. The Mercer brothers know what they're doing. And if there's even a chance they could help us, we'd be foolish not to take it.

I sigh. "Okay, fine. But you have to do the talking."

"Ivy." Her tone changes. "Stop saying shit like that. You know this business inside and out. Hell, it took me four years of college to learn what you've picked up from reading over contracts and talking to our lawyer."

"You're right. But still, I'll let you take the reins since you're the one who suggested it in the first place."

Tessa grins and picks up her phone, typing out a message. My heart pounds as I watch her hit send, half hoping he won't reply. But barely ten minutes later, her phone dings.

I freeze, my hand clutching a spoonful of batter.

"He says he'd love to meet! Tomorrow at three at their office. Oh shoot..." Tessa's face falls as she glances at her calendar. "I totally forgot—I have that meeting with Suzette."

I swallow hard, the realization sinking in. That meeting with the real estate agent is equally important. I resign myself to my fate, once again seeing Asher Mercer. "I'll go. I promise, I can handle it."

Tessa's smile returns, bright and hopeful. "You've got this, Ivy. Besides, it's just Asher."

Just Asher. If only it were that simple.

CHAPTER 2
ASHER

"Are you going to that party at Tilt?"

I squint, staring at the cars that look like toys on the street down below. When I don't hear an answer, I look back over my shoulder, my brother completely oblivious to my question.

"Guess not," I mutter to myself, turning my attention back to the view from the window.

My office overlooks the city, the snow-covered Chicago skyline stretching out like a picture-perfect postcard. The afternoon sun reflects off the glassy buildings, casting everything in a soft, wintry glow. Normally, I'd lose myself in the view, but today, my mind keeps wandering back to the message I got earlier.

Tessa Marlow, of all people. Her cherubic face pops into my head, all my memories of her still from high school. It's been years since I saw her last, but apparently, she and lifelong friend Ivy Calloway are opening a bakery and looking for my advice.

It's been a while since I thought about those days. Tessa was always sweet and friendly, the type of person who had a kind word for everyone, even a guy like me who didn't always deserve it. I find myself wondering what she's been up to since then, how life has treated her.

I glance back over at my brother, Zane, who's pacing around my office with a stack of notes in his hand, looking like he's about to wear a groove into the floor. I chuckle, memories of him trying to pretend he wasn't checking Tessa out when she was round popping in my head. "Hey, guess who reached out to me?"

He barely looks up, focused on whatever calculations he's running through in his head. "Who?"

"Tessa Marlow. She wants to catch up and talk about a new business she's starting with her friend." He stops in his tracks, his movements pausing at the mention of her. A name I'm sure he hasn't heard for almost ten years—one that I know brings a rush of memories back to him, even if he'll never admit it.

Zane snorts, finally looking my way. "Old high school buddy, huh? What's she need—investment advice? Or just hoping to rub shoulders with the Mercers?"

I roll my eyes at his usual cynicism. "Maybe a little bit of both. But come on, we've been in their shoes. It wasn't that long ago we were hustling to get this company off the ground. Plus, she and her friend have been running a side baking business for years. I looked into it—they've got potential based on their strong social media presence and the extensive reports she sent over. I just have to see if the numbers are there. I would love if you would go over them as well since you're the numbers guy."

He stops his pacing, leaning against my desk, a smirk playing at the corner of his mouth. "Her friend... Ivy, right? The quiet one?" he asks, completely ignoring my other comment.

I shrug, keeping my expression neutral even though the mention of her name sends a jolt through me. "Yeah, I think so. Why?"

Zane raises an eyebrow, his smirk widening. "No reason. Just curious."

I shake my head, but my mind drifts back to Ivy anyway. Back in high school, she was different—edgy, smart, and focused on things far outside the football field social circle I ruled. While I was busy with practices, parties, and being crowned prom king, she was buried in books, lost in her own world. We barely interacted, but I always noticed her. She was the kind of girl you noticed, even if she never realized it.

She had this way of moving through the halls, head down, a look of determination on her face like she had more important things on her mind than high school drama. She didn't care about fitting in or being liked, and maybe that's what intrigued me. I admired that about her—maybe even envied it a little. She had this quiet, *I don't give a fuck about your opinion* way about her. But back then, I was too caught up in my own image to do anything about it.

Zane watches me for a moment longer, his gaze too knowing for my liking. I clear my throat, pulling my thoughts back to the present. "Anyway, I told Tessa we could meet tomorrow afternoon."

"Kind of fucked up to be thinking about a girl you went to high school with at your age."

"Jesus." I roll my eyes, his boisterous laugh echoing around us. "You're fucked up, you know that? I was just remembering what she looked like; the only memory I have of her is from high school."

"Still trying to get up the nerve to talk to her?"

"Why do *you* remember her name? You're the older brother; you were barely even around when we were in high school," I remind him, the only time we ever really crossed paths as students together in high school was the off chance we bumped into each other in the hallway when he bothered showing up, or the few times Mom made him give me a ride.

"We both know why I remember her—" He smirks and for a second, I think he's going to say something about his not-so-secretive crush on Tessa. "Ivy was the one girl who scared you growing up."

"I wasn't scared of her," I clarify, feeling a touch defensive. "She was best friends with Tessa, whom I thought had a crush on me, so I wasn't about to fuck that up."

It's a lie. He knows it; I know it. The truth was, I was terrified of a girl like Ivy in high school. The smart ones who had their shit together always saw through my facade and, sadly, not much has changed.

At twenty-eight, I thought I'd have my personal life just as figured out as my professional life, but to date, that couldn't be further from the truth. The last three dates I've had ended with zero promise. One ended with me dropping the woman off at a club to meet up with her friends and the other two... I let my dick do the thinking—one turning into a *friends with benefits* thing and the other telling me she thinks she's in love with me after two hookups which left me having to break her heart that the feeling wasn't mutual.

His movements pause, his gaze still focused on the paper in his hand for a few more seconds before he chuckles. "Whatever you say, little brother." Then he just shrugs and heads back to his office, leaving me alone with my thoughts—and that uncomfortable flicker of anticipation I can't quite shake.

"Michelle, can you send me the report that shows how we did Q4 last year?"

I'm in the middle of a conference call, going through the latest financial reports, when I hear a knock on my office door.

"Of course," Michelle replies. "I sent them over to Zane last week but I'll forward them to you as well."

I glance at my watch—time completely getting away from me.

"Your three o'clock is waiting," Keri, my assistant, whispers, tapping her wrist. It's not often she has to walk in and physically remind me to hang up the phone but with year-end right around the corner, business never sleeps.

"Sorry, everyone, I have to drop. Thanks again for your time." I hang up, standing from my chair and buttoning my suit jacket as Keri steps aside, widening the door.

"He's ready for you now." She smiles toward the person behind the door, then steps aside, ushering for her to step in my office.

"Good afternoon," I say preemptively, "I'm sorry I ma—"

I expect to see Tessa, with her bright smile and easy demeanor, but when the door swings open, it's not her.

It's Ivy.

For a second, I just stare. She's changed—or grown up rather. She still has that alternative edge, but there's a subtle confidence in her stance that wasn't there before. My mind instantly flashes back to her in high school, her shoulders up to her ears, her eyes cast down as she practically scurried down the hall to her next class. She was shy, that was obvious, but there was always something so much more behind those eyes, some far-off look like she was already planning out her life five years ahead of the rest of us.

Her hair, once kept just beneath her chin, is long, dark, glossy, and straight, falling over one shoulder, and she's dressed in a sleek dark-green coat that brings out the warmth in her hazel eyes. Those eyes, the ones that always seemed to see more than anyone gave her credit for, flick up to meet mine, and I'm caught off guard by the way my heart stumbles in my chest.

I clear my throat, pasting on my easygoing smile. "Ivy, hey. I-I—" I chuckle at myself stumbling over my words. "I'm sorry I kept you waiting. It's been a long time." I extend my hand toward her. "Where's Tessa?"

She hesitates, then steps farther into the room, and I catch the faintest hint of vanilla and cinnamon as she moves to clutch my hand with her own. Her skin is warm, her touch so gentle I look down to make sure she's actually touching me.

"She had a last-minute meeting with our real estate agent, so I'm here instead." She tucks a loose strand of hair behind her ear, her fingers brushing her neck. "I hope that's okay." Her voice sounds familiar; it's definitely still Ivy's somewhat monotoned cadence but there's a maturity to it now, an almost whisper-like rasp to it.

"Of course. Sorry, I just meant that I was expecting to see her—I'm pleasantly surprised that it's you." I gesture to the chair across from my desk, trying to ignore the way my pulse kicks up a notch when her fingers gently pull back from mine. "Have a seat, please. So, you two are starting a bakery?"

Ivy sits down, smoothing her hands over her coat, and I notice the way she bites her lip before answering, like she's weighing every word. "Yes, technically. We've actually had this baking business for some time. So taking the next steps of getting a brick and mortar bakery, well, it's been in the works for a while now." She smiles hesitantly. "When Tessa mentioned speaking with you and your brother, we both thought it could be beneficial. So, thank you for taking the time." Her fingers nervously tap against her leg. She is wearing black tights beneath the coat, her feet encased in Dr. Martens boots.

"Happy to." I smile back at her. Her eyes shift slightly away from me, then bounce right back. There's still a hint of that shy young girl from days past, but she squares her shoulders, clearing her throat like she's fighting it. "How far are you along in the process?"

"Pretty far. We have a building we'd like to put an offer on and we're in the final stages of the pre-approval process." Her movements are rigid, her answers sounding programmed.

"Hmm, pretty far is right, then." Her fingers stay interlaced in her lap and I can't help but wonder if she's excited at all. "Tell me more about it, Ivy." I settle my eyes on her, hoping my openness will allow her to feel more at ease. I lean back in my chair, my posture relaxing as my tone becomes more engaging. I want to know everything about her, what she's been up to the last decade, if she's happy, what she's doing after this. But I don't ask those questions. Instead, I keep it professional. "What made you want to open a bakery? What's your specialty? Is baking your passion?"

"Oh." Her shoulders relax a touch, a smile starting to spread across her lips. "Actually, it's been a dream of ours since college. We

—er, I started baking as a hobby, a way to channel some energy into something other than school and it just grew from there."

"I can't imagine needing other things to keep me busy in college," I share. "I was lucky to get the bare minimum done between parties." I laugh at the confession, then suddenly feel immature. Ivy doesn't strike me as the type who ever partied. I think I saw her at one, maybe two in high school, and that was only because of Tessa, I'm sure.

"I was usually in the science lab." She blushes. "Chemistry major."

"Chemistry?" I whistle. "I knew you were smart but damn."

"It was fun." She shrugs with a small laugh. "Plus, it translated to baking very well."

"So, you're the baker?" I ask, changing the subject. She nods enthusiastically, her natural demeanor peeking through more and more. "What are you going to call it—the bakery?"

"Sugar & Spice."

"Cute." I chuckle and a pink blush creeps up her delicate neck. My cock instantly stirs, my brain wondering how far that blush goes down her chest. I wince at the thought, guilt creeping in. This isn't a woman in a bar I'm attempting to pick up; this is Ivy Calloway—a woman who wants my input, not my dick.

"So you said you've been running this business for years. Did it start in college?"

"Thanks, and yes, we've actually been running this holiday cookie business out of my apartment for years, and we finally decided it's time to make it official. Well, technically—"she gestures, her movements growing more confident—"I started it by making holiday cookies in my dorm during finals to relieve stress, which led into cookies for big game days when I would bake too many or someone's birthday." She sighs. "And then the frat boys found out and unknowingly blew up my business by telling all their friends while they smoked weed."

"Really?" I laugh, my head falling back as I picture a group of stoned-as-fuck frat boys banging on her door, begging for cookies.

"Yeah." She rolls her eyes. "It was a crazy time which is why I roped Tessa into helping me."

"They ever get you to smoke with them?" I joke but her cheeks flush again. "Oh? Little Miss good girl Ivy Calloway smoked weed in college?"

"I never said I did." She smiles, attempting to keep a straight face before bursting into laughter. "Okay, okay, maybe once or twice but it made me too hungry. I was eating my baking supplies so it wasn't going to work."

I'm laughing so hard my belly hurts at this point. "Well, shit, I never imagined you breaking the rules at all, let alone the law."

She shrugs, a playful smirk on her face. "I guess I grew up a little in college."

"I guess you did." I don't mean for the words to sound seductive, but they do. I also don't mean for my eyes to linger on hers, dropping down to her perfectly shaped lips either, but they do.

"Once we both saw the kind of money we could make from it, we decided to try and do it every year, making enough money that we were both able to pay down a significant amount of our student loans before we even graduated. And the best part was—is—we both love it; it's truly our dream."

"Damn, sounds like Zane and I could have probably taken some advice from you two when starting our business."

"I doubt that." She blushes again, tucking her hair behind her ear. "You two seem to be light-years ahead of us... which is why I'm here."

"Well, I'm glad you're here." I smile. "Apart from any advice I might be able to give you, it's nice to see you again and reconnect." Her eyes shift nervously away from mine for a second and I worry I've been a little too bold. But something tells me that the energy I'm feeling between us goes both ways. "How have you been otherwise?"

"Good." She nods. "Pretty focused on the business up till now, so not much has changed for me since college. You?" I watch her throat constrict as she swallows; she's nervous.

I wonder if this our way of each of us trying to sniff out if there's a significant other in each other's life. "Good." I nod, our eyes lingering on each other. "Pretty focused on work as well." I laugh. "Actually," I admit, "completely focused on nothing *but* work sadly."

"I guess what they say is true, then—you have to be willing to make sacrifices for what you really want."

"I'd say that's pretty accurate, but I'd like to think it won't be this way forever—for either of us." Her smile is slight, her hands nervously tangling with each other again. "Anyway," I say, sitting more upright in my chair, "back to your business. Tell me about your recipe process. I'm curious how you went from chemistry to baking."

Her eyes light up again, her expression becoming more animated as she launches into a twenty-minute monologue all about her process, how she discovered her love for it, and her favorite flavor profiles.

She's passionate about it—I can see it in the way her eyes light up when she talks about their recipes, how she leans forward just a little when describing the concept for their bakery. It's infectious, and I find myself wanting to know more, to ask her a thousand questions about the flavors and the process, about what drives her, what makes her happy, how she likes to spend her spare time, if she ever wondered about me all these years the way I wondered about her.

Instead, I focus on keeping things professional, turning the conversation to the details of their business plan.

"And you've been profitable since the start?" I ask, impressed.

"Yes. We've kept track of all of our financials meticulously over the last five years. I think Tessa sent them over to you along with our business proposal? She manages the business side of things mostly, but we both go over the numbers, budgeting, the ROI, etc. so that we're on the same page."

"She did and I spent some time going over them last night, not too in-depth but enough to get an understanding of where you stand." I nod, leaning back in my chair. "You've got some strong ideas here and the numbers to prove it. You obviously don't have a problem with the baking aspect, getting repeat customers and rave reviews. And you both understand it's smart to expand on what you've already built, not making it too complicated. And your niche —traditional recipes with a twist—has potential. But..."

I see her tense, bracing herself for criticism, and I have to fight back a smile, wanting to tell her to relax, that she's most likely being too hard on herself just like she was in school. Even now, she's so serious, so determined to prove herself.

"But what?" she asks, her voice carefully controlled.

"You're underestimating your projected costs. Chicago isn't cheap, especially if you're looking to set up in the neighborhoods you're targeting. Rent, marketing, permits—those numbers add up fast. And the competition is fierce. You'll need to differentiate your-selves, build a brand that people can't ignore."

She's quiet for a moment, her brow furrowing as she considers my words. Then she nods, a small, determined smile pulling at her lips. "You're right. It's something we're still working on. But we're ready to put in the work. Tessa's handling the marketing side, and I'm focusing on the recipes and like I said, both of us helping with operations. It's a good balance."

There's a fierceness in her tone that catches me off guard, and I realize she's not just trying to convince me—she's trying to convince herself. It makes me soften, just a little. I know that struggle, of trying your hardest to believe in what everyone else sees in you, even when you're struggling to see it yourself.

"Well, you've got my attention," I say, leaning forward. "I think you two might have more than just a shot at this. I think you're going to be wildly successful."

Her eyes widen slightly, like she wasn't expecting that, and I find myself wondering how many times she's been underestimated. Probably a lot, considering how many people overlooked her back in high school. I feel a flicker of guilt, remembering how I never made an effort to know her better back then, always too wrapped up in my own world.

Ivy shifts in her seat, glancing out the window before turning her gaze back to me. "It's still hard to believe sometimes. Tessa and I used to joke about opening a bakery when we were up until three a.m. decorating cookies in our cramped college apartment. Now we're actually doing it."

I nod, my curiosity getting the better of me. "You two have always been close, haven't you? I remember you being pretty inseparable back in high school."

She smiles softly, a wistful look crossing her face. "Yeah, she's... she's been my best friend since we were kids. Honestly, I don't think I would've made it through high school without her dragging me to all those games." She blushes, her eyes drifting from mine briefly. "And a few parties." She glances at me, a touch of amusement in her eyes. "I think you were at most of those, weren't you?"

I chuckle, rubbing the back of my neck. "Yeah, I guess I was. It's kind of embarrassing to think about now, but back then, it felt like the most important thing in the world. Football, prom, being the life of the party."

There's a pause, a moment where something unspoken hangs between us. She's watching me carefully, like she's trying to decide if she should say what's really on her mind.

"You seemed... happy," she says finally, a softness in her voice. "Confident. Like you had everything figured out."

I let out a low laugh, shaking my head. "You'd be surprised. Turns out, playing a part and actually knowing what you're doing are two different things."

She blinks, clearly surprised by my honesty, and for a second, the distance between us feels smaller. She opens her mouth, like she's about to say something, but then she catches herself, looking down at her hands instead.

I realize suddenly that I don't want her to feel like she has to hold back. Not with me. "You know, our company is throwing a holiday party in a few days," I say, trying to keep my tone casual even though my heart is pounding a little too fast. "You and Tessa should come. It'd be a good chance to network, meet some potential investors, maybe even show off a few of your cookies. I know I'd love to taste them."

She hesitates, her pink cheeks glowing again and I can see the wariness in her eyes, the way she's weighing her options. I hold my breath, wondering if I've pushed too far, if I've misread her completely. But then she nods, offering me a tentative smile.

"I'll talk to Tessa. Thanks for the invite, Asher."

I nod, feeling a strange sense of relief, but also... something more. Something I don't want to name yet. As she stands and gathers her things, I can't help but watch her, wondering what she's thinking, if she's as surprised as I am by this unexpected connection.

She reaches for the door, hesitating for a moment before glancing back at me. There's a question in her eyes, one she doesn't quite ask, and I find myself wishing she would. But then she just nods again, a little awkwardly, and slips out of the room.

As the door clicks shut behind her, I let out a breath I hadn't realized I was holding. My mind is spinning, filled with thoughts of Ivy Calloway—how she's different now, yet still has that quiet intensity that used to draw my attention even when I pretended not to notice.

And for the first time in years, I find myself wondering if maybe the guy who peaked in high school could have a second chance to prove himself. Maybe this holiday season has more surprises in store than I thought.

CHAPTER 3

IVY

The cold wind bites my cheeks as I step outside the Mercer building, tugging my coat tighter around myself against the sharp Chicago air. Snowflakes swirl around me, sticking to my hair, but I barely notice. My mind is a whirlwind of thoughts, each one louder than the last. I focus on the rhythmic crunch of my boots on the snow-covered sidewalk, trying to ground myself, but it's no use. My mind keeps circling back to one thing—no, one person.

Asher Mercer.

Seeing him again, after all these years, sent those familiar butterflies dancing through my lower belly, reminding me why I had that silly little crush on him all those years ago. He's changed, but in a way that only makes him more intriguing. Back in high school, he was all easy smiles and effortless charm, but now there's a depth to him, a seriousness that wasn't there before. It's like he's grown into the person everyone expected him to be, and I can't help but wonder if he's truly happy.

And yet, some things about him are the same. That smile, for one. I tried to stay focused during our meeting, but every time his lips curled, making his eyes crinkle, that familiar swooping feeling tugged at my stomach, just like it used to when I was seventeen. I told myself back then that he was just a teenage crush, that I was only drawn to him because he was everything I thought I wasn't—confident, popular, the person everyone wanted to know. But now, I'm not so sure.

I let out a shaky breath, watching it billow out in a cloud of white, and shake my head, trying to regain some sense of control. This is just business—strictly professional. And yet I can't ignore the flicker of something that I haven't felt in a long time, something that feels a lot like hope, but also excitement.

My fingers curl inside my gloves, pressing against my palms as I quicken my pace. I can't peel the smile from my face as I replay the way his eyes lit up as they scanned my body. While my thick wool coat doesn't give away much about my shape, I can still tell when a man has to actively stop himself from letting his eyes linger.

But as soon as I giggle out loud to myself, I remember his invitation to the holiday party and my stomach drops. Not only do I not have anything to wear to an event the Mercer brothers would put on, but I'm way out of my league if it means having to steal his attention away from a crowd of people.

"I just won't go," I say to myself with a shrug as if it is as simple as that. I take the stairs down to the train to head back to my place, my head now completely drowning in everything Tessa and I have to do next for Sugar & Spice.

Back at my apartment, the warmth hits me as soon as I step inside, along with the comforting scent of cinnamon and sugar. Tessa is perched on the edge of the couch, her laptop balanced on her knees as she types away, no doubt refining our business proposal for the hundredth time. She looks up when she hears me come in, her eyes lighting up with curiosity.

"Well? How did it go?" she asks, closing her laptop and setting it aside. Her voice is casual, but I can tell from the way she's leaning forward that she's dying to hear every detail.

I shrug, trying to keep my expression neutral as I hang up my coat. "It was fine. We went over the business plan. He gave us some feedback."

Tessa arches an eyebrow, a knowing smirk playing at her lips. "Just fine? What'd he say?"

"I took detailed notes," I say, pulling my notebook from my bag. I tug my hat off, running my hands through my hair to untangle the wet clumps of snow still hanging on. "He pretty much said we're doing everything right, but we should reevaluate our cost analysis."

"What?" She grabs the notebook from me and flips through the papers. "Which pricing was off? Did he say specifically?"

"No." I shrug. "Why?"

"Because he's wrong. I ran the numbers a hundred times at least and I used actual cost metrics based on our business over the last five years."

"Okay," I say, holding up my hands at her defensiveness. "Any chance you could be wrong? He is the wildly successful entrepreneur and multimillionaire, remember?"

"No." She's already back on her laptop, eyebrows knit together, tapping furiously.

"Anyway, I'm sure we can go over it with the lender, but um, yeah, that's it." My gaze nervously flicks away from hers when her eyes shoot up over the laptop to look at me.

Shit. Why do I always have to give myself away?

"That's it?"

"Yeah, that's it. I think he mentioned that we could reach out at any time with other questions." She narrows her gaze at me. "What?"

"Really? That's it? Because you look like you've seen a ghost—or, you know, a guy you've been secretly crushing on for a decade, and now you're acting weird."

"I'm not being weird—I just," I attempt to protest, to come up with a lie on the fly, but it's no use. I'm a shit liar and I know my face is lobster-red right now. "He asked us to his company holiday party. He said we could go over things further there."

"You were going to hold out on me?" She squeals, hopping up from her seat. "Or wait, did he invite *you* to the holiday party to 'discuss things further' or did he invite *us*?"

I feel my cheeks heat up, and I busy myself rearranging the cookies cooling on the counter. "It wasn't like that. He invited *us* to their holiday party... said it would be a good networking opportunity. And I didn't agree that we'd go because it's something you and I need to discuss and agree on—if we have time with everything else going on."

"Oh, I bet he did," Tessa says, standing up and crossing the room to join me by the counter. "Did he look at you with those smoldering eyes of his and flash that signature smile? The one that's supposed to make everyone fall at his feet?"

I let out an exasperated sigh. "Stop it, Tess. He was just being polite. It's not a big deal. And he was completely professional."

"Uh-huh. Sure. And I'm Santa's little helper," she says with a teasing wink, nudging me with her elbow. "Come on, Ivy. You've got to admit, it's kind of exciting. Seeing him again, after all this time... Maybe there's a little spark?"

I bite my lip, hesitating as I reach for a cookie. "It's just... he's different now. I'll admit, he's still charming and all, but there's something else. Like he's... I don't know... grown-up." I glance at Tessa, wondering if I'm making any sense.

"You mean intimidating."

"Yes," I say emphatically, "very intimidating."

"Is that why you never went for him in school?"

I sigh, not wanting to relive those days. Not because I didn't have a great time but because it just reminds me how little I believed in myself back then... or hell, even now.

"And what if I did ask him out now? If he's single, that is, what if he still only sees me as Tessa's shy friend? The weird, quiet girl who was always third-wheeling with you."

Tessa's teasing grin fades, replaced by a more thoughtful expression. "Is that what you think of yourself, Ivy?"

My shoulders sag a little and I know whatever she's about to say to me is right, that my perceptions of myself are merely a reflection of my insecurity. I know all these things, yet I still find myself sabotaging my own attempt at finding happiness.

"Not really, I don't think. I know us, our friendship has always been real. I know you didn't take me around out of obligation. I think it's just easier to believe those things than believe in myself."

She slips an arm around my shoulders, pulling me into a side hug.

"You're not the same girl you were back then, Ivy. You're stronger now. You're a badass baker with a business plan that's going to knock the bank's socks off. Me and you are going to launch this bakery and within a year, we're going to be so damn busy there are gonna be lines around the block on the weekends. And besides, who cares what Asher Mercer thinks? This is about us and our bakery."

"Oh, so now it's *who cares what he thinks*?" I laugh. Her words make sense, and I nod, trying to let them sink in. But there's a part of me that can't let go of the fear that I'll always be that quiet girl in the background, the one who blended into the scenery while Tessa lit up every room she walked into.

"He's a guy, what does he know?" She takes a sip from her smoothie, rolling her eyes with a casual wave of her hand dismissively. "Clearly, not as much as us; my pricing isn't wrong." Then she pauses, slowly placing her cup back onto the counter. "Wait a minute. Maybe he suggested our pricing was off because he knew it would make you worried so then you'd have to go to his party to talk to him further!"

"Okay, I think you might be watching a little too much true crime because that's insane." I change the subject, hoping she won't press me further on the Asher conversation. "Anyway, did you hear back from Suzette?"

She rolls her eyes, taking the bait. "Yeah, she's still trying to sell us on that overpriced spot on Milwaukee Avenue. I told her it's out of our budget, but she won't give up. I swear, it's like she thinks we're made of money."

"I think they do that because there's always room for nego-tiation."

"I just get annoyed. Like in *House Hunters* when they tell the agent their budget is absolutely no higher than this and fifteen seconds later, they're showing them a house that's eighty thousand dollars over budget. Like, what the hell?"

One of the things I love most about Tess is, there's never a ques-tion on how she feels about something. Either her facial expression or her tongue is going to tell you.

"It's not like we can just say, '*Oh, let me reach into my back pocket for that extra money for the down payment.*'" She reaches for her laptop again and holds it up. "Anyway, let's go over the proposal one more time."

"Again? Forty-seventh time's a charm?" I laugh softly, grateful for the distraction. But as I settle onto the couch next to her, my mind drifts back to the way Asher's hand brushed mine as he handed me his business card, the way his voice softened when he said, "*You've got potential,*" like his words meant so much more than what he was actually saying.

Maybe I'm reading into it and maybe I imagined the way his eyes took me in, but I know I didn't imagine the spark that ran between us when we touched.

It's a memory that makes my stomach flip, no matter how hard I try to push it away.

I LIE IN BED STARING AT THE CEILING, LISTENING TO THE DISTANT HUM OF THE city beyond my window. Sleep doesn't come easily, not with my thoughts tangled up in the past. I remember the way I used to sneak glances at Asher in the hallways at school, how my heart would race whenever he walked by with that easy, confident stride of his. He was always surrounded by people—football buddies, cheerleaders, kids from every social circle who seemed to worship him.

And I was... well, invisible. Except when I was with Tessa, who had no problem dragging me into every social event she could. She was the one who'd nudge me toward Asher at parties, whispering, *"Just go talk to him,"* while I tried to hide my nerves behind a red plastic cup.

I never took her advice. I convinced myself that he wouldn't care about a girl like me—someone who spent more time in the library than at pep rallies and parties, who preferred studying to cheering at football games. I kept my crush safely locked away, content to admire him from afar, where he couldn't disappoint me.

The bell rings, echoing down the hallway, and the air fills with the sound of shuffling feet and chatter. I try to blend in, slipping my textbooks against my chest like a shield as I weave through the crowd. My pulse picks up, and my eyes scan the hallway, searching.

Then I spot him.

Asher's walking down the hall, a lopsided grin on his face like he doesn't have a care in the world. He's wearing that worn-out letterman jacket with his name stitched on the front, and his dark hair is tousled just right, like he rolled out of bed that way—effortless, perfect. There's this energy that surrounds him, magnetic and impossible to ignore. He's the kind of guy everyone knows, the one people naturally gravitate toward. I swear, it's like he carries the sunlight with him, and everything else is just drawn in.

I know I shouldn't stare. But I can't help it.

He's surrounded, as usual. Football buddies in their jerseys, cheerleaders with high ponytails and perfect smiles, a couple of kids from the drama club—even teachers give him nods and smiles like he's some kind of local celebrity. And maybe he is. In a small town like ours, someone like Asher—quarterback, honor roll, friendly with just about everybody and comes from a just as good-looking and well-to-do family—feels like he's at the center of everything.

I duck my head, pretending to be busy with my locker as he approaches. The metal is cool beneath my fingers as I twist the dial, but my hands shake a little, and I fumble the combination. I'm acutely aware of the way my heart pounds, a steady thrum in my chest that feels embarrassingly loud. I tell myself it's stupid, that he's just a guy—a guy who probably doesn't even know my name. But even so, every time he walks by, I feel the same rush, the same thrill, like I'm on the edge of something big and unknown.

I sneak another glance just as he's passing by, his laughter ringing out, clear and warm. He's got this easy, confident stride, and I think that's part of what draws me in. He moves like he owns the space around him, like the world is always going to bend in his favor. I wonder what that must feel like—to walk through life with that kind of confidence, to know people want to be near you just because you exist.

And then, as if he can feel my gaze, he looks up. For a second, our eyes meet, and my breath catches. His eyes are a deep, warm brown, and there's this softness there, a hint of curiosity. It's just a split second, barely enough time for my mind to register that yes, he's looking at me. Me.

"Hey, Ivy." That smile widens and my knees actually tremble like I'm about to end up in a jumble on the floor.

He does know my name.

I suck in a sharp breath, my lips parting slightly as I muster just enough courage to answer back. I'm just about to say it. But then someone claps him on the shoulder, and he's pulled back into the throng of people.

The moment is gone, like a bubble bursting. I turn back to my locker, pretending to search for a book I don't need. My face feels warm, and I know if anyone sees me right now, they'll notice the flush spreading across my cheeks.

I replay the moment in my head over and over, savoring it even though I know it's nothing. Just a look. Just a second. But it feels like more. It feels like proof that maybe he's noticed me, too.

I know it's silly. I know he's the kind of person who belongs to everyone, who lights up rooms and makes people feel special with a grin. But I can't help the way my heart races when he's near or the way I find myself searching for him in every crowded hallway.

And I can't help but hope that one day, he'll look at me like I'm the only person in the room.

But today, standing in his office, I couldn't shake the feeling that things were different. The way he looked at me—like he was really seeing me for the first time—it was enough to crack open those old, carefully buried feelings. And now, no matter how much I try to tell myself that it's just nostalgia, that it's just a silly high school crush resurfacing, I can't deny the flutter of hope in my chest.

THE NEXT MORNING, I'M IN THE KITCHEN EARLY, MIXING UP A FRESH BATCH of cookie dough. Baking is my therapy, my way of quieting the noise in my head, and right now, I need it more than ever. I lose myself in the rhythm of the process—the soft scrape of the wooden spoon against the bowl, the scent of brown sugar and butter filling the air.

But just when I'm starting to find my calm, Tessa strolls in, still in her pajamas and dragging her feet.

"Slept over again, I see."

"Yeaaaaah." Her answer morphs into a yawn and then a stretch as she reaches for a mug from one of my cabinets. Ever since we committed to opening this business, it feels like any extra second we have is spent traveling between our apartments so it's not uncommon we just crash at each other's place.

She leans against the counter with a mischievous grin on her face, cradling a mug of coffee in her hands. "So, I've been thinking about the party."

I narrow my eyes at her, already suspicious. "Oh, have you?"

"Yep." She takes a sip, her expression annoyingly smug. "And I've decided that we're going."

I stop mid-stir, turning to face her. "We? Tessa, I thought we agreed that this was a maybe. You know, if we weren't too busy with the bakery and all."

Tessa shrugs, unfazed by my protests. "Yeah, well, I decided to change my mind. Think about it, Ivy—Asher's right, it's a great chance to network. We could meet potential investors for expansion opportunities, make connections, and besides, Asher invited us. It'd be rude to say no."

"Uh-huh, and what happened to he's just a guy, what does he know? Blah, blah, blah." I roll my eyes, crossing my arms. "You just want to play matchmaker."

She grins, not even trying to deny it. "Okay, fine, maybe I do. But come on, you can't seriously tell me you're not the least bit curious to see what happens. Who knows? Maybe this is fate giving you a second chance."

A second chance. The words send a shiver down my spine, and I grip the edge of the counter, trying to steady myself.

"Tessa, it's not that simple. He's... he's Asher Mercer, successful entrepreneur, like I said. We reached out to him for help, not for me to try and redeem myself from high school."

"You're Ivy Calloway," she interrupts, her voice firm. "You're smart, you're talented, and you've built something amazing with me. Stop acting like you're still that shy girl from high school. You're a woman of the world. You've been through some things; you know who you are now. And fine, forget fate. Maybe you just need to be fucked?"

"God." I shake my head at her crassness... but she's not wrong. "You have such a way with words; maybe I should just say that to him."

To say that things have been stirring since I saw him would be quite the understatement. More like the faucet's been turned on full blast and I'm worried I'm about to lose control of it like a fucking fire hose.

"Trust me, that would be the one surefire way to seal the deal with him." She laughs.

I swallow hard, feeling the familiar tightness in my chest. That same tightness I always get when it comes to the idea of putting myself out there and being vulnerable. "I just... I don't want to get my hopes up, okay? What if he's just being nice? What if he doesn't see me as anything more than a former classmate he's helping with her business?"

Tessa sets her coffee down, her expression softening as she steps closer. "Look, Ivy, I know you're scared and I know I've made a lot of jokes about you and Asher, but if you really are still interested in him, outside of just physical stuff, then the only way you're going to know if he wants anything more is to get to know him. Sometimes you've got to take a chance, even if it scares the hell out of you. And if it doesn't work out, well... at least you'll know, right?"

Her words hang in the air, filling the silence between us, and I let out a shaky breath. Deep down, I know she's right. I've spent so long holding myself back, afraid of what might happen if I let anyone in. But maybe it's time to stop hiding, to take a risk, even if it means facing the possibility of rejection.

I look at her, seeing the hope in her eyes, and finally, I nod. "Okay. Let's go to the party." Tessa's grin is so wide it almost splits her face. "Oh shit, I don't have anything to wear."

"Yes, you do!" she says. "Remember that little black dress I convinced you to buy last year?"

I had actually completely forgotten about that dress. I shake my head at the thought of wearing it. "That was *way* too sexy for a work party."

"Exactly, they'll be so dazzled by your beauty they'll gladly want to invest."

"But for business purposes like you said." I point toward her to drive home my seriousness. "And if Asher and I happen to spend time talking about personal things, then so be it."

"And don't worry, you'll see once you put that dress on. It's going to be amazing."

I force a smile, but my heart is still pounding, a mix of excitement and dread swirling in my chest. As I watch her buzz around the kitchen, already planning our outfits, I try to convince myself that this is just another business move, a chance to make connections and grow our dream. But deep down, I know this decision is about more than just the bakery.

It's about seeing Asher again, about finding out if the spark I felt in his office was real or just a figment of my imagination. And as much as it terrifies me, I can't shake the feeling that this holiday season might be my chance to finally be that cliché person who says exactly what's on their mind and in their heart, expecting a miracle.

My office is perched high above the city, a wall of windows offering a perfect view of Chicago's skyline, glittering beneath the afternoon sun. I stare out, tapping a pen against the desk as I try to focus on the spreadsheet in front of me. But my mind keeps wandering to her. A notification buzzes on my phone, and I glance down to see a message from an unknown number.

UNKNOWN

Hey, it's Ivy. Tessa and I will be at the party. Thanks for the invite.

I lean back, a smile tugging at the corner of my mouth. Ivy Calloway. I can't say I expected to hear from her, but I'm not complaining. Seeing her at the office the other day was like flipping through an old yearbook and finding the one photo you always lingered on—nostalgic, but somehow still a stranger. She's different now, and yet I could still see that shy girl trying so hard to take over her confidence.

I type out a quick reply.

ME

Glad to hear it. Looking forward to catching up. Is it just you and Tessa?

It's a simple enough question, but I can't help the curiosity. I know Ivy was always the quieter one between the two of them, always hanging back while Tessa lit up every room she walked into. Back then, it was easy to overlook her. Now, it's impossible. But that's not where my curiosity lies. I fully expected her to come along; I just wasn't sure if I should expect a date on her arm.

There's a pause before her reply comes in, and I find myself staring at the phone like some teenager waiting for a message. I let out a small laugh at myself—a man on the verge of thirty shouldn't be acting like this. But the truth is, Ivy's different. Always has been, I was just too stupid to notice.

IVY

Yep, just the two of us. Tessa's already planning our outfits, so there's no backing out now.

I grin, imagining Ivy reluctantly getting dragged into whatever plan Tessa has cooked up. I send another text.

ME

Good. I wouldn't want you to back out. Besides, I'm sure you'll look amazing.

I don't know what I'm expecting—a playful response, maybe even a little banter—but there's a thrill in waiting for her reply. It's a little reminder that, no matter how much I've achieved or how successful I've become, there are still things that make my pulse race in ways no amount of money ever could.

Her reply pops up after a moment:

IVY

Don't get your hopes up. I'm not really up on party attire but Tessa has promised to make me presentable. I promise, I'll be in something other than black jeans and a black sweater.

I chuckle, picturing Ivy in her usual low-key outfits she wore in high school, something about her that hasn't seemed to change. She was never one for the spotlight, which makes me wonder how she handles working alongside Tessa, who always thrived on it, like me. Then again, maybe that's why their dynamic worked so well.

Instantly, I'm left wondering how she'd do in my life. The spotlight of business, social media, politics, and everything else always on me. I knew going into this business that was a small price to pay for everything that comes with success. But I've also realized along the way, through my own heartache, that some people want nothing to do with a life like mine and no amount of love can overcome it.

I push the thoughts aside, sending a response back.

ME

As my guest of honor, I can't wait to see what Tessa comes up with. But if you ask me, you'd stand out in anything.

I contemplate sending something else, something not so subtle about just how fucking sexy I actually find her, but decide against it. I'm trying to be a different man, trying not to lead with the one thing I'm confident I don't have to try with—sex.

I toss my phone onto the desk, forcing myself to focus on the spreadsheet in front of me. It's the quarterly earnings report from Michelle I'd requested during our meeting. The numbers are strong, the growth projections even stronger. Mercer Enterprises is set to have another record-breaking year, and as the face of the company, I have plenty of interviews, press conferences, and investor meetings lined up to keep it that way.

All the things Zane hates doing. I can't help but compare me and him to Ivy and Tessa. I smile, thinking about how similar Tessa and I were in high school—outgoing, loud, the center of attention. And then there was Zane, lurking in the shadows, keeping to his angry self.

Shit, maybe I should try and hook those two up.

There's a knock at my door. Keri steps in, a tablet in hand and a serious look on her face.

"Mr. Mercer, *Forbes* wants to confirm your availability for an interview next week. They're doing a spotlight feature on young CEOs and their impact on local communities."

I nod. "Set it up. Make sure we highlight the new program we're launching with the local schools—internships and mentorship opportunities."

She types a note on her tablet. "Got it. Also, the *Wall Street Journal* is requesting a statement on the recent acquisition. They want to know how you plan to integrate the new tech into our existing platforms."

I rub the back of my neck, glancing at the email notification on my laptop. There's always something, always someone looking for a quote or a soundbite. "Draft a response for me to review, but keep it focused on growth potential and synergy. Investors need to see that this move is going to pay off long-term."

Keri nods and exits, leaving me alone with the steady hum of business as usual. I know the drill by now. Ever since Zane and I turned Mercer Enterprises from our parents' struggling manufacturing business into a tech and media empire, the spotlight's been relentless. We're the golden boys of Chicago's business scene—the Mercer brothers, a brand in and of itself. I can't count how many times I've been on the cover of *Crain's Chicago Business* or how often my name pops up in the local news.

From Small-Town Quarterback to Tech Titan, one headline read last month. And another read, **Asher Mercer's Rise to the Top —Chicago's Favorite CEO Speaks Success and Strategy.** I should be used to it by now. I know how to smile for the cameras, how to answer the reporters' questions, how to play the part of the young, charismatic leader with a vision.

And yet lately, I've felt a little off. Like I'm watching my life from the outside, going through the motions but missing something real. Maybe it's the endless events or the way the press expects me to always be "on." Or maybe it's because, when I look at all the articles and news clips, I see someone polished, someone the public expects me to be. And the truth is, I don't know if that's really me anymore.

Neither is my personal life that's been splashed through the tabloids over the years as well—decisions I'm not so proud of.

I glance down at my phone again, Ivy's message still open. I'm used to people seeing me as a CEO, as the guy who can turn a company around and land million-dollar deals. I'm used to it being business, not personal.

But with her, it felt different. In that meeting, when she talked about the bakery, there was a passion in her eyes, a realness I haven't felt in a while. I remember when I had that same passion, before it only ever became about numbers. For the first time in months, it felt like I wasn't just Asher Mercer, CEO. I was just Asher, sitting across from a woman who looked at me like I was still the same guy she remembered from high school. A guy she felt comfortable enough with to ask for advice but wasn't there to pitch me something.

I lean back in my chair, staring out at the skyline. Ivy and I never really crossed paths back then—sure, I noticed her, but I was too wrapped up in football, parties, and my own ego to make a move. She was always there, though, on the edge of things. I wonder if she knows I remember her, that I noticed the way she'd sit alone with a book or how she'd quietly laugh at something Tessa said.

My phone buzzes again, pulling me from my thoughts. It's a news alert.

Mercer Enterprises CEO Asher Mercer Set to Expand Youth Mentorship Programs Across Chicago.

I shake my head, swiping the notification away. Sometimes it feels like all the headlines are just noise. I know the work we do is important—Zane and I built this company to be more than just another tech giant. We wanted to create something lasting, something that would give back. But the media frenzy that comes with it is exhausting.

I remember the simpler days when the biggest thing on my mind was getting through a football game or passing my next math test. Things were clearer then—straightforward. Now, everything's wrapped up in appearances, numbers, and managing perceptions. There's no room for mistakes.

Keri comes back in, her expression more urgent. "Asher, the *Chicago Tribune* wants a statement on your rumored involvement with the mayor's initiative for tech hubs in low-income neighborhoods."

I let out a slow breath. "Tell them we're committed to supporting local communities and providing resources, but that we're not ready to make any formal announcements."

She nods, and as she leaves, I think about how this life—this whirlwind of meetings, press releases, and interviews—is exactly what I signed up for. I built this, and I take pride in it. But lately, I can't help wondering what else is out there.

My phone buzzes again, and this time it's Ivy.

IVY

> Thanks for the vote of confidence, but I'm not sure about being the 'guest of honor.' Don't want to steal your spotlight.

I grin, the tension in my chest easing a little. There it is again—that playful honesty.

I type back:

ME

Trust me, Ivy, I could use a break from the spotlight. It's nice to have someone around who's not just trying to get a headline with me.

IVY

Shoot. Guess I'll have to pass now since my plan has been foiled.

I laugh out loud when I read her quick response.

She's going to be fun.

As I set the phone down, I feel that familiar tug—like maybe there's something more here than a chance reconnection. Maybe, for once, I can just be myself around someone who doesn't see me as the rich CEO who has to perform—around someone who I want to be myself with.

Maybe I want that more than I realized.

CHAPTER 5
IVY

My apartment twinkles with the soft glow of Christmas lights strung across my bookshelves and the small tree Tessa and I picked up last weekend when I dragged her to the local Christmas tree lot down the street. It's cozy in here, the kind of atmosphere that's supposed to be soothing. But instead, my mind is a chaotic mess, tangled with nerves about the Mercer holiday party tomorrow.

I sit cross-legged on the living room floor, surrounded by a sea of wrapping paper, ribbons, and half-wrapped gifts. My hands fumble with a roll of silver ribbon, but I'm too distracted to manage a decent bow. The idea of being at that party has my stomach in knots, and I can't seem to shut off the anxious thoughts running through my head.

Tessa claims it'll be good for us—a chance to network with people who might help make our bakery dream a reality. And I know she's right. But it's not just the thought of making small talk with potential investors that has me on edge.

It's Asher.

"Come on, you're making that face again," she says, flopping down beside me and nudging me with her shoulder.

I glance at her, trying to act casual. "What face?"

She arches an eyebrow, giving me a knowing look. "That face. The one you make when you're overthinking something to death. What's got you so worked up?"

I shrug, not meeting her eyes, focusing on the ribbon in my hands instead. "It's just... the party. I'm not sure I belong there." I fidget with a piece of wrapping paper, smoothing out the wrinkles that don't actually exist. "You should have seen his office, Tess, and him..." Her eyes grow wide. "You could smell how expensive he is, not to mention that his suit had to have been custom and his watch —probably a Rolex or something."

Tessa's expression softens, the teasing fading from her eyes. "Look, I know you're nervous, but just be yourself. You don't have to impress him or anyone else. Who gives a shit if he's a gazillionaire? He's still just Asher Mercer from high school, right?"

I nod, trying to absorb her words, but my chest still feels tight with uncertainty. This is the part of business that terrifies me, the rubbing elbows with important people and trying to convince them you deserve their money or even worse, their business. "It's just... I don't know if I'm ready for this. And we do have to impress people if we're looking to network and find investors or whatever. What if I mess up or say something awkward or—"

Tessa lets out a snort, cutting me off. "Ivy, you have literally faced down furious college professors, tricky yeast doughs, and Chicago traffic during rush hour. I think you can handle a holiday party. Oh, and that insane lady who had a rat on a leash in the train that one time; she was terrifying!"

I let out a shaky laugh, despite myself. "Yeah, I guess you're right."

"Besides," she reassures me. "That's my job. I'm the face of the bakery, the business side of things. And you know I never shut the hell up, so trust me. I can handle schmoozing some rich folks. You just focus on having a good time and hanging out with Asher."

"But I still don't know what I'm supposed to say to him. We

barely knew each other back then, and now it's like... I don't even know if he remembers me at all. It feels stupid to reminisce about high school when we have basically no memories together and I have zero idea what a big-time CEO even talks about." I can feel my throat tightening again, my anxiety getting the better of me.

Tessa pulls back slightly, looking me straight in the eye. "He remembers you, Ivy. Trust me. Guys like Asher don't invite you to parties for no reason. And besides, this is amazing; you have a blank slate with him. You guys can flirt, do that super sexy touching of his arm, flick your hair, press your tits together!" I laugh, that anxious feeling melting into excitement. "That is arguably one of the most fun and sexy times with a guy—the talking phase." She swoons.

"Really?" My nose scrunches. "I always felt like it was the most stressful time. Trying to relate and find things to talk about; you know I stress about small talk. Most people don't want to talk about quantum or atomic theory and I really am not interested in hearing about another man's investment portfolio."

"Did I teach you nothing?" She scoffs before jumping up dramatically. "Remember in high school when I'd tell you to watch me when I walked over to Darren Thompson and he'd just melt in a puddle of goo at my feet—that's what you need to channel at this party with Asher."

"Uh, that was like ten years ago and I'm pretty sure tying a cherry stem into a knot with my tongue isn't going to impress him."

"Not that." She grabs my arms and maneuvers me so I'm standing in front of her. "I'm talking about when you're engaging with him, lean in." She shows me, her eyes softening as she smiles like she's laughing at something I've said. "Touch his arm, like this." She demonstrates, then cocks her head. "Make him think you're hanging on every word he's saying. Guys eat that shit up."

"The problem isn't that I can't remember this stuff, Tess. I've seen all the rom-coms too. The problem is I get in my head and clam up because I'm either overthinking or I trip, stumble, and then swan dive into an unrelatable topic of such insane proportions the guy sneaks out of my apartment when I get up to go the restroom."

"You brought out a model of an atom, Ivy."

"It was a polyhedron molecular model actually."

"Not the point."

"Right." I sigh. "I really don't want to be alone forever, I swear. I just feel like I've completely lost myself along this bakery journey. Not that I don't want it, it's my dream. It's just—I guess I naively didn't realize just how much of it would consume me to the point I feel like I'm just existing."

It feels good to finally admit that out loud.

"I'm sorry, Ivy." Tessa's face softens and we sink down to the floor, talking like we did when we were sixteen. "I didn't realize you felt that way. At times I wondered if you were avoiding the world, seeing you lock yourself away and work on recipes and concepts while also trying to give your job one hundred and ten percent."

"I think it happened subconsciously. I know I'm safe in the kitchen, safe in a book—but I've never met someone I felt safe enough with to truly be myself and not feel like I'm always putting on a show of what they want to see."

"Ah, shit. I'm sorry, I didn't mean to imply that with my little lessons about flirting."

"No, no, I know that. It's me. I'm the one who gets in my head. I convince myself it's easier to just stay in the lane I know rather than see what else is out there. And as much as I don't want to admit it..." I smile at her. "Us being together twenty-four seven has also given me an out to not seek companionship elsewhere."

"Yeah, I've had that realization too." She bumps against my shoulder. "Kind of hard for any man to compare when your best friend is your soul mate. But you have to make room for yourself this year; you have to let me do more so that you can find yourself again. You deserve that. We both deserve that."

Her words hit me in a way I wasn't expecting, and for a moment, I can't speak around the lump in my throat. I blink back the sudden prickle of tears, swallowing hard before I manage to reply. "Thanks, Tess. I don't know what I'd do without you."

She squeezes my shoulders, her grin returning in full force. "Lucky for you, you'll never have to find out. Now, come on—we have to figure out what we're wearing tomorrow. You can't just show up in your usual sweater-and-jeans combo. It's time to break out the big guns."

I raise an eyebrow, trying to keep up with her sudden shift in tone. "Big guns?"

She hops to her feet, practically bounding over to my closet. "The little black dress I convinced you to buy last year. The one you swore you'd never wear because it was 'too sexy.' Well, tomorrow night, it's making its debut."

Dammit, I completely forgot I do have something to wear... technically.

I shake my head, but a small smile tugs at my lips. "Tessa, I don't know... it's just a party. And I'm not sure a little black dress is exactly me."

She waves a dismissive hand, already rummaging through my closet. "Nonsense. You'll look amazing. Besides, you said it yourself —this is a chance for us to network, right? We need to make a good impression. And that starts with showing up looking like a million bucks."

I hesitate, watching her pull the dress from the back of the closet, holding it up with a triumphant grin. It's sleek, elegant, the kind of thing I'd never have picked out for myself, but as I study it, I feel a flicker of curiosity. Maybe stepping out of my comfort zone wouldn't be the worst thing in the world.

"Okay," I say finally, taking the dress from her hands, "but if I look ridiculous, I'm blaming you."

Tessa just grins, giving me a playful salute. "Blame away. But trust me, Ivy, tomorrow night is going to be the start of something great. For the bakery, for us... and maybe even for you and Asher."

I roll my eyes, but I can't quite squash the tiny thrill of hope that flutters in my chest. Maybe she's right. Maybe this party is the begin-

ning of something new and maybe wearing this dress is the first step
I can take toward finding myself.

THAT NIGHT, I LIE AWAKE, STARING AT THE SHADOWS THAT THE CHRISTMAS
lights I've left on in my window cast on the ceiling. I think about
Tessa's words, about the possibility of a fresh start, and I try to
picture what that would even look like. I've been so focused on work
and building this business the last few years that I haven't given
myself the chance to stop for even a second to ask what I want.

Asher. That's what I want.

That familiar flush creeps up my neck, and my thighs beginning
to rustle restlessly beneath the sheets. An aching need has settled
between my thighs the last few days. I squeeze tighter, my hands
wandering down my body to find release. My skin is warm, hot even.
My pulse quickens, my breath picking up as my fingers slip over my
clit.

I'm so primed that within a minute or two I'm gasping, my whispered moans breaking the silence. I kick my blankets from my body,
the soft breeze from my overhead fan a welcome reprieve.

I wonder if Asher is thinking about me—if he's thought about
me while stroking himself. The thought scares me as much as it
excites me.

I think about the moments in his office—his smile, the way he'd
seemed genuinely interested in our bakery plans, the way his eyes
had lingered on mine a second longer than necessary. I want to
believe that it meant something, that maybe he sees me differently
now, but I can't quite bring myself to hope too much.

What if I'm just reading into things that aren't there? What if
he's only inviting us because he feels obligated or because he's trying
to impress Tessa? The doubts twist in my chest, making it hard to
breathe. A sickening feeling rushes through me as I think that maybe

he was into her all these years and that's why his face conveyed his shock when I walked into his office.

It was disappointment, not excitement.

But then I remember the way he'd leaned in when he spoke to me, how he'd listened when I talked about our recipes with that intense focus that made me feel like I was the only person in the room. I can't help but hope there's a chance I'm not imagining things.

I close my eyes, letting out a slow breath as I try to calm my racing thoughts. Tessa's right—I've faced plenty of challenges before, and I've always come out stronger. Tomorrow is just another step, another chance to show myself what I'm capable of. And maybe, if I'm lucky, it'll be a chance to show Asher too.

As I finally drift off to sleep, I hold on to that thought, letting it warm me like the glow of the Christmas lights.

THE NEXT DAY PASSES IN A BLUR OF LAST-MINUTE BAKING AND FRANTIC preparation, with Tessa fussing over every detail of our outfits like it's the damn Oscars and not just a corporate holiday party. I barely have time to breathe before I find myself standing in front of my bathroom mirror, smoothing out the dress that hugs my curves in a way that makes me feel both exposed and... powerful.

"Holy fucking shit!" Tessa gushes. "You look like a sexy Morticia Addams!"

The black silk lies gently across my breasts that are on prominent display in the corset top. I suck in another breath, my waist looking impossibly narrow with the magic of this dress. I turn to double-check my profile, doubt starting to creep in.

"I don't know." I turn in the mirror, looking at the way the sheen of the material accentuates my shape. "It feels like it's too much."

Tessa beams at me from the doorway, her own dress shimmering in the low light. "You look incredible, Ivy. Stop overthinking it. He's not going to know what hit him."

I take a deep breath, willing myself to believe her. "It's just a party," I remind myself, trying to keep my voice steady. "I'm doing this for us. For the bakery."

"Of course you are," Tessa says with a sly grin, "and if a little holiday magic happens along the way, well, who's going to complain?"

I laugh, the sound coming out more nervous than I intended, but Tessa just squeezes my hand and leads me toward the door.

"I might need some champagne to make that magic happen."

As we step out into the cold night, my heart races with a mixture of nerves and anticipation. I tell myself that this is just another step toward our future, but I can't shake the feeling that tonight might be more than that. That maybe, just maybe, it's a chance for a new beginning. For the bakery, for us... and for me.

"Hey," Tessa says, grabbing my hand as we ride the elevator to the top floor of the high-rise building. "Let this night be fun. I know we want to network but we also know that we can do this, even without the Mercer brothers' connections."

"You think so?" I ask, suddenly so nervous my stomach feels like it's in my throat.

"Are you kidding me?" She laughs, adjusting her dress and pressing her tits up so her cleavage is more prominent. "Please." She scoffs with that confidence I envy so much. "If boys can be successful in business, how hard can it be?"

The elevator doors glide open, and I step out into the glittering lobby of the Mercer high-rise. Everything is bathed in the soft glow of twinkling lights, gold and silver decorations draped over every surface.

Giant crystal snowflakes hang from the ceiling, spinning slowly, while festive garlands snake around the pillars and a tree that's at least twelve feet tall stands in the center of the room. The scent of pine mingles with the faint, sophisticated aroma of hors d'oeuvres. The noise of laughter and clinking glasses washes over me, and my nerves flare up again, tightening my chest.

I smooth my hand over my dress, trying to ignore the way my stomach flips as I take in the crowd of elegantly dressed people. At least my fear of being overdressed is no longer a concern. The luxury dresses and custom tuxes make me feel like I'm crashing a party I was never invited to. Tessa, of course, looks like she belongs here, her shimmering silver dress catching the light as she strides confidently beside me.

"Wow, this is... something," I murmur, glancing around at the lavish decorations and the sleek, high-ceilinged space, trying not to feel like a complete fish out of water.

"It's a lot, but you're going to be fine," Tessa whispers back, looping her arm through mine and giving my hand a reassuring squeeze. "Come on, let's find Asher and Zane. Remember, we're here for business, Ivy." She gives me a wink. "Just talk business; you're confident as hell in our plan."

"Right." I nod, but my voice comes out weaker than I'd like. Tessa leads us into the thick of the party, weaving through the clusters of guests. I try to steady my breathing, but the second my eyes land on Asher across the room, my mind goes blank.

He's standing near the bar, surrounded by a group of well-dressed guests, all of them laughing at something he just said. He looks like he's stepped out of a holiday magazine—black suit, perfectly tailored, his hair neatly combed but with just a hint of the boyish tousle that made him so effortlessly charming back in high school. There's a warmth in his smile as he chats with his guests, but when his gaze shifts and locks on mine, something changes in his expression. It's as if a spark jumps between us, and for a moment, I feel like he's seeing me—not just the quiet girl from high school, but the woman standing before him now.

Asher's smile falters, then transforms into something more genuine, less polished. He says something to the people around him, excusing himself from the conversation, and starts making his way through the crowd toward us. My breath catches in my throat as he draws closer, his eyes never leaving mine.

Tessa's grip on my arm tightens, and she leans in, whispering playfully, "Breathe, Ivy. You've got this."

But I don't feel like I have this at all. My heart is hammering in my chest, each beat echoing in my ears. Tessa gives me one last encouraging smile before Asher reaches us, and then she releases my arm, letting me stand on my own.

"Ivy, Tessa, you made it." Asher's smile is wide, but there's something else in his eyes as he looks at me—something curious, maybe even a little nervous. His gaze lingers, sweeping over my breasts before meeting my eyes again. I feel heat rising to my cheeks when his eyes darken and drop back down to my breasts, lingering long enough to not just be a casual glimpse.

"We wouldn't miss it," Tessa says, her voice light and teasing, "especially not with such great company." She nudges me subtly, a gesture that's far from subtle.

Asher's eyes stay on me, his smile softening. "It's good to see you here, Ivy. You look..." He clears his throat. "Fucking incredible."

I let out a small, nervous laugh, trying to deflect the compliment. "Thank you."

"Sorry, I just... that was unprofessional but... shit." He gestures toward me. "Yeah, I stand by it; you look fucking incredible."

I laugh nervously. My stomach does about sixteen backflips and I'm confident my face is a record setting shade of red. "I think I might be a little underdressed compared to everyone else," I say, gesturing around at the sea of black-tie attire.

His gaze doesn't follow my hand movement, remaining focused

on me. He leans in slightly, his voice dropping just enough that only I can hear him. "Trust me, nobody is noticing a fucking thing except you in that dress."

His words send a shiver through me, the low tenor of his voice pulling me in. Instead of wanting to disappear into the ground beneath his intense gaze, I feel the desire to lean in a touch closer, my body swaying just an inch.

For a moment, the noise of the party fades into the background, and it's just the two of us, standing there in the glow of the Christmas lights, the air between us buzzing with something I can't quite name.

Tessa clears her throat dramatically, and I snap back to the present, taking a step back. "Oh my God. Sorry. Asher, you remember Tessa?" In my excitement to see him again, I completely forgot that they haven't seen each other or even spoken yet.

"Excuse me." He extends his hand toward her. "That was rude of me. Tessa, so great to see you again. I was just admiring Ivy's dress."

"I know, right? A total smoke show and to think she almost didn't wear it." She laughs, flashing me a quick *I told you so* look "And it's great to see you too." She shakes his hand confidently. "Thanks again for inviting us and for talking about our business plan."

"Of course. I'm so happy you two could make it. I had a great conversation with Ivy. I'm sure she told you about it when she got back. Sorry I kept her so long. I think we talked for what—three hours?" he asks, looking over at me.

"Um, yeah." I blush, Tessa's brow lifting slowly when he reveals just how long I was at his office, a little detail I may have left out when we reconvened later that day. His eyes shoot back to me and that nervous smile I can't seem to hide slides back into place. It's like there's a little hidden secret being exchanged between us.

"Well, I'm going to grab a drink," Tessa says, all but winking at me. "I'll leave you two to... catch up. Asher, we'll talk later."

Before I can protest, she's gone, disappearing into the crowd with a knowing smile. I feel a rush of both annoyance and gratitude toward her—annoyance because she's left me alone with Asher, but gratitude because... maybe I don't mind being alone with him.

Asher's gaze follows Tessa for a moment, then returns to me, an apologetic smile tugging at his lips. "I think she planned that."

"She definitely did," I reply, managing a small smile of my own. "She's not exactly subtle."

He chuckles softly, running a hand through his hair, making it look even more perfectly tousled. "She hasn't changed much, has she?"

"No," I say, my smile growing a little, "she hasn't."

Asher pauses, studying me with an intensity that makes my heart flutter uncomfortably. "And what about you, Ivy? Have you changed?"

The question catches me off guard, and I'm not entirely sure how to answer it. I shift my weight, suddenly feeling self-conscious under his gaze. "I don't know. I guess... maybe I've grown up a bit. Learned to take more risks." The last part is more of a thing I intend to do.

"What kind of risks?"

"Well, opening a bakery for one."

"That's a big one."

"What about you, Asher? I imagine you're not exactly the same guy from high school either."

He smiles, but there's a shadow behind it. "Yeah, I guess a lot has changed. Turning a company into an empire will do that to you. Shit." He shakes his head. "That sounded douchey as hell."

"No." I laugh, my hand darting out to touch his arm softly, my eyes immediately looking down to see where my fingertips are resting on him. I almost pull them back but Tessa's little trick from the other night comes back to me and I let my fingers linger. "I get what you're saying. It would be silly not to consider how running a multimillion-dollar company could change you or your perception of the world."

His eyes struggle to stay focused on mine, dropping just as I pull my hand back, my fingers dragging slowly down his arm and over his wrist as I pull back. "I bet it's a lot of pressure. Keeping up with the company, making sure everything runs smoothly while also being in the spotlight?"

"Yeah, it can be. But it's... worth it, I think. I'm not one of those people who wants to pretend that their privileged life is harder than anyone else's. And it's nice, every once in a while, to be reminded of where I came from because it is easy to let it all go to your head, get blinded by it all, and lose sight of what's really important."

I tilt my head, curiosity bubbling up despite my nerves. "Is that what this party is for? A reminder?" He glances around, understanding I'm referring to the lavish extent to which this place is decorated and the piles and piles of presents with his employees' names on them.

He shrugs, but there's a wry smile on his lips. "Maybe. Or maybe it's just an excuse to throw a fancy party and pretend I know what I'm doing."

I laugh softly, and the tension between us eases a little more. "Well, you're doing a pretty good job of pretending."

He grins, and for a second, it feels like we're back in high school, trading easy smiles across a crowded room. But then his expression shifts, turning more serious, more uncertain. He takes a step closer, his voice lowering again. "Ivy, I've been thinking about our meeting. About what you said and the bakery."

My pulse quickens, and I brace myself, unsure of where this is going. "Oh? And what did you think?"

He hesitates, his expression earnest. "I think you and Tessa have something really special. And I want to help you make it happen, if you'll let me."

The offer catches me off guard, and for a moment I can't speak. "What do you mean? In what capacity?"

"I want to be an investor. I know you're already working with a lender and we can get my finance people on with them so that it wouldn't drag things out further or screw up any offers you might have already."

I blink several times, my mouth still hanging open. "Uh, um, no... no offers yet."

"With my investment, you and Tessa could keep your cash liquid, really lean into marketing, and let Tessa not be financially cuffed by such a tight budget that you are currently operating under."

"Thank you, Asher," I manage, my voice softer than I intended. "I'm not sure what to say— Tessa, I should talk with Tessa, though."

"Of course, absolutely." We stand there in silence for several seconds.

He holds my gaze, and for a heartbeat, the air between us is charged with something unspoken, something electric. I can feel the heat of him, the way his presence seems to fill the space around us, and I'm suddenly very aware of how close we're standing. If I reached out, I could touch his chest, feel the warmth of his skin through his shirt. The thought makes my breath hitch.

"Ivy—" he starts, but before he can finish, someone claps him on the shoulder, pulling him away.

"Asher, my man! Great party!" A tall, smiling man ambles up to us, oblivious to the moment he's interrupted. He extends his hand, and Asher's expression shifts back to the polished smile he was wearing when I spotted him across the room earlier.

"Thanks, Mike. Glad you could make it," Asher replies, though his eyes flick back to me, an apology in his gaze.

I take a step back, trying to hide the disappointment that surges through me. "It's okay," I murmur, managing a smile. "Go ahead, do your thing."

He hesitates, like he wants to say more, but then he nods. "I'll find you later, okay? Don't leave without saying goodbye."

I nod, but as he's swept back into the crowd, I can't help feeling like the moment we shared is slipping through my fingers. I turn away, searching for Tessa, but my mind keeps replaying the way

Asher looked at me, the way his voice softened when he spoke my name.

I make my way through the glittering crowd, trying to ignore the flutter in my chest and the undeniable urge to turn around and look back at him one more time.

CHAPTER 6
ASHER

The holiday party hums around me—laughter, the clinking of glasses, the murmur of music mixing with the buzz of conversation. But none of it matters right now. The moment I step near the Christmas tree, all I see is her. Ivy, standing in the soft glow of the lights, the colors playing over her dress, casting shades of gold and red that make her look... radiant. Her hips gently flare out away from her cinched waist.

I lean against the wall, trying to look casual. It's easier than admitting that she makes me nervous. She always has. But I don't let it show. Instead, I focus on her, my attention sharp, like she's the only person in the room worth looking at. And right now, she is.

"I told you I'd find you," I say, stopping a foot behind Ivy, my voice dropping an octave.

"Hey." She spins around, a smile already stretching her dark cherry-colored lips. "You didn't have to. I know you're busy."

"Nah, they're all drunk. Nobody cares about me right now." I cross my arms, trying to play it cool even though my heart is racing. I shake my head with a nervous chuckle, sliding my hands into my pockets to keep them from reaching out to grab her waist.

"I wouldn't say *nobody*," she teases with a little roll of her eyes.

"Listen, I wanted to. Ivy, I..." I trail off, running a hand through my hair, feeling almost uncertain all of a sudden. Like I'm about to cross a professional boundary that could complicate things. "I know we've reconnected professionally and I think there's a strong future there, but I'd be lying if I said I wasn't curious—beyond that."

She blinks, clearly caught off guard by the honesty in my words. "Oh."

"I never really got to know you back in high school, did I? At least nothing beyond just... seeing you with Tessa or a casual hello in the hallway."

"No, I guess not. I don't think I ever gave you a reason to, did I?" she replies, her voice barely above a whisper. "I was always too busy hiding in the library, but I wasn't hiding from you or anyone. Well, maybe I was—"

"No, nothing you did," I clarify.

"Maybe you were just busy too." She shrugs.

I take a step closer, her eyes searching mine. "Maybe. Or maybe I was just too busy being the guy everyone thought I was supposed to be."

"Meaning?" She looks up at me, my height making me tower over her, even in her heels.

"Meaning you're a breath of fresh air." I reach out slowly, brushing a soft curl away from her neck. "Or maybe just a lovely reminder of what life could be like."

I worry I've said too much when my eyes meet hers again. They're wide, searching mine like she's suddenly treading water without land in sight. "So, I have to admit," I start, letting a teasing smile slip onto my face, hoping my change in tone lightens the mood, "you're not quite what I expected—now, I mean."

Her eyebrow arches, and she crosses her arms over her chest, but there's a flicker of curiosity in her eyes. "Oh? And what did you expect, Mr. Mercer?"

That look for one.

I can't help the chuckle that escapes me. "I remember you as the girl who always had her nose in a book. The quiet one. I thought you'd be... I don't know, more uptight."

She laughs softly, and the sound hits me right in the chest, mingling with the music around us. "So you thought I'd be boring?"

"No, not boring. Just... maybe a little more reserved. Less likely to show up at a party like this." I gesture to the crowd—a sea of people in designer suits and cocktail dresses, all looking like they belong.

"Well, you invited me."

"I was going to say show up to a party like this, in that dress." I nod toward her tits. "Not to mention that snarky little attitude you've developed."

She follows my gaze, then meets my eyes again with a smile that's half-amused, half-challenging. "To be fair, I've always had the attitude; you just never had the pleasure of experiencing it."

"Is that so?" I shake my head, the tension between us growing so thick my cock is begging for attention. "Damn shame on my part."

"The tits are new, though; they grew in during college."

"Fuck me." I laugh, dragging my hand down my face, hers glowing red. "I take it back; you are absolutely able to hold your own at this party."

"Honestly, though? I'm not that comfortable with all of this. But I've learned that pretending to be confident sometimes works just as well as actually being confident. Fake it till you make it or whatever."

"You fake it, huh?" I shake my head, clicking my tongue. "I never would've guessed." She tilts her head, giving me this look like she's assessing whether that was an innuendo or not. "And yes," I continue, deciding to leap past any and all professional boundaries I was second-guessing a moment ago. "I meant that exactly as you're thinking I meant it."

She looks at me for a few more seconds, that flush from her cheeks reaching down to her neck. I watch her throat constrict as she swallows and I want to reach out and wrap my fingers around it. She's contemplating taking the bait, on taking it further.

"It's all an illusion. Smoke and mirrors. Or in this case, a little black dress."

"You know, I like this side of you, Ivy. It's... exciting."

She raises an eyebrow, that playful spark still in her eyes. "Of course you do, it's designed to excite you. Biology."

"Mmm, God, I love nerdy talk then, because biology has me very, *very* excited." I laugh.

"Trust me, if I started in with the hardcore nerdy talk, you'd be gone before I could say thermonuclear dynamics."

I smirk, leaning in just a fraction. "Well, you do have a way of charging up my ions."

"A cation."

"A what?"

"That's an ion with a positive charge, a cation." She flushes, and it's hard not to feel a thrill at the way her cheeks go pink, but the real thrill is hearing her laughter fill the space around us. "And what about you, Asher? You're not exactly what I expected either."

That catches me off guard, and I can't help but tilt my head, intrigued. "Oh yeah? How so?"

"I thought you'd be—" She pauses, and I watch her search for the right words. "I don't know, more... full of yourself."

I wince dramatically, but I keep the grin on my face. "Ouch. I'm not sure if I should be offended or flattered you felt you could be honest with me."

"Maybe a little of both?" she teases, and there's something in her smile that makes me want to keep this conversation going, to dig a little deeper. "I just didn't expect you to be... real, I guess. You were always so put together in high school, like you had everything figured out. And obviously, you and Zane have done some pretty incredible things in the ten years since we graduated."

I shrug, feeling a touch of something I rarely let show when it comes to my personal life—honesty. "Turns out, I'm realizing that most of that was just an act. It wasn't that I didn't like playing football or being involved in everything, I just never gave it a second thought. The pressure was there and I just fell into the trap of living up to it. Guess we've both been faking it, huh?"

"Maybe." She leans back against the wall beside me, and the warmth from the Christmas lights dances across her face, making her look even softer, even more... tempting. I try not to get too lost in the way she looks right now, like she's someone I could spend hours talking to and never get bored. The reality is, we don't know each other anymore and never really did. She's a reminder of home, of that small-town life when things felt so much easier.

There's a pause between us, just the faint hum of the party and the soft glow from the tree filling the space. For the first time tonight, I'm not thinking about all the people I need to impress or the business associates I'm supposed to schmooze. I'm thinking about Ivy and the way she's looking at me, like she's waiting for something.

"You know," I say, almost without realizing it, "I always wondered what you were reading back then. When you sat in the bleachers during football practice. You looked so... focused."

She blinks, and for a moment, she looks surprised—maybe even a little shy. "You remember that?" she asks, her voice softer, almost like she can't believe I paid attention.

I nod, my eyes not leaving hers. "Yeah, I remember. I used to think you were reading something profound—like Tolstoy or Nietzsche. Something serious and poetic."

She laughs, and the sound is light, almost like music. "Oh God, no. It was definitely not Tolstoy. It was probably some mystery novel or maybe... fantasy. With dragons and sword fights."

I can't help but feel delighted. I didn't expect that answer, but it fits her in a way I didn't realize until now. "Fantasy, huh? Why doesn't that surprise me?"

She crosses her arms, but there's a hint of a smirk on her lips. "What can I say? I've always liked stories where the secretly fierce heroine wins in the end."

I lean closer, letting the warmth of her words sink in. "Ivy

Calloway, lover of dragons and sword fights. I never would have guessed."

She shrugs, but I can tell she's hiding a smile. "Well, I never would've guessed that Asher Mercer, star quarterback and prom king, would be interested in our little bakery. Yet here we are."

I laugh, shaking my head. "Touché. But in my defense, it's not every day that I meet someone who can turn baking into a science."

She lights up at that, like I've just said the magic words. "Baking is science," she insists, and I love how her eyes brighten when she talks about it. "It's chemistry, thermodynamics, molecular gastronomy..."

I raise an eyebrow, feeling genuinely entertained. "Molecular gastronomy, huh? That sounds pretty intense for cookies."

She waves me off, but her smile is infectious. "Hey, don't knock it. If you get the wrong ratio of flour to liquid, you'll end up with a cookie that's either too dry or one that spreads out into a sad, shapeless puddle. It's all about finding the right balance. You know, kind of like life."

Something about that sticks with me, and I lean in even closer, feeling like we're sharing a secret. "So what's the secret to finding that balance, then? In baking—or in life?"

Her eyes flicker with something—maybe confidence, maybe a challenge. "That's the thing. There is no perfect balance. It's all a little trial and error. You add a little too much sugar, maybe a little more flour, see what happens. If you're lucky, you end up with something delicious. If you're not, well... you try again. And sometimes, you might discover something completely new that you never even considered in the first place."

"I think I like that philosophy, Ivy. I'll have to keep it in mind the next time I screw up a batch of pancakes. Maybe I'll accidentally make crepes for the first time and end up loving them."

She raises an eyebrow, her smile turning more teasing. "You cook?"

I put my hands up in defense. "Okay, maybe 'cook' is a strong word. Let's just say I'm capable of feeding myself without burning down my apartment."

She laughs, and it's the kind of laugh that makes me want to hear it again and again. "I'd like to see that. Maybe you could come by the bakery sometime. I'll give you some pointers before you accidentally poison yourself or burn down the building."

The idea of spending more time with her sends a thrill through me. I grin, leaning back a little but keeping my eyes locked on hers. "Deal. I'll bring the wine."

For a moment, it's just the two of us. Everything else fades—the music, the crowd, all of it. Her expression softens, and there's a warmth in her eyes that makes my heart pick up speed. I can't help but think that I missed out on something back in high school. "You know, Ivy," I say quietly, "I know I said it earlier, but I missed out on something back in high school. Not getting to know you."

She looks up at me, and there's something honest in her gaze. "You never really looked, Asher. And I guess I never gave you an opportunity."

I take a step closer, feeling a pull I can't explain. "Well, I'm looking now."

The air between us feels charged, like everything could change in the next second. For a moment, I think maybe I'll reach out, maybe close that last bit of space between us. But before I can, someone bumps into me from behind, and the moment shatters. I catch myself against the wall, laughing as a tipsy partygoer stumbles past.

I glance back at Ivy, feeling the moment slip away. "Looks like the universe isn't ready for us to test that theory yet."

She smiles, but I can see the disappointment, just a flicker before she hides it. "Maybe it's a sign," she says, her voice light but her eyes saying something else, "or maybe I'm just too much of a control in this experiment."

I grin, trying to lighten the mood. "Well, I guess that means I'll just have to keep looking for an opportunity."

Her cheeks flush a little, but she doesn't look away, and there's a spark in her eyes that tells me she's just as caught up in this as I am. Before I can say anything else, Tessa appears at her side, holding two champagne flutes and looking like she knows exactly what she's interrupting.

"Here you go, Ivy," Tessa says, thrusting a glass into Ivy's hand. "Thought you could use a drink."

She's all smiles, her eyes flicking between the two of us, and it's obvious she's enjoying herself. "Am I interrupting something?"

I glance at Ivy, waiting for her to say something, but she just shoots Tessa a look that's half-annoyed, half-amused. I can't help but laugh, shaking my head. "Not at all. Ivy and I were just... catching up."

Tessa grins, looking far too pleased with herself. "Oh, I'm sure you were. Well, don't let me keep you."

She disappears into the crowd, leaving me and Ivy alone again. I watch her go, then turn back to Ivy, who's staring down at her glass like it's the most interesting thing in the world. "Your friend is... quite the character," I say, raising my glass in a mock toast.

She lifts her own glass, a small smile on her lips. "You have no idea."

"And what about you? I'm afraid I don't know as much as I'd like."

We clink glasses, and I take a sip, but I don't take my eyes off her. She meets my gaze over the rim of her glass, and for a moment, it feels like we're in our own little world again, everything else fading into the background.

"You know, Ivy, I think I'd like to change that. Maybe get to know more about what's behind that scientific mind of yours."

I watch as her eyes soften, and there's something vulnerable in her expression that makes my chest tighten. She doesn't look away, doesn't put up her usual guarded smile. Instead, she holds my gaze, and I can tell—she's letting me in, even if it's just a little.

"Well," she says, leaning in slightly, her voice playful but with a hint of something deeper, "if you're looking for more baking chemistry lessons, you know where to find me."

A slow smile spreads across my face. "I might just take you up on that."

There's a charge in the air between us, something electric. I feel it, and I know she feels it too. I take a small step closer, letting our shoulders brush, and the warmth of her skin against mine sends a thrill through me. "Okay, but don't expect any shortcuts," she says, her eyebrow quirking up. "Perfecting a recipe takes time and patience. And a willingness to get your hands a little messy."

I lean in, feeling the pull of her words, and I can't help the grin that forms. "I'm good with my hands," I murmur, my voice low. I watch her face go pink, and there's something about seeing her flustered that makes me want to push just a little further. Makes me wish I could reach down and pull her dress away from her body to see if the flush matches her nipples.

She swallows, trying to keep her composure, but I can see the way her eyes flicker, the way her breath catches. For a second, I think about closing that last bit of distance between us, about what it might feel like to just let this happen. But before I can decide, someone calls my name from across the room, and it breaks the moment.

I glance over and see one of my business associates waving me over, looking impatient. I sigh, a pang of frustration settling in my chest. I don't want to walk away from this, from her, but I know I have to. "I have to take care of this," I say, the reluctance clear in my voice.

She nods, and I catch a hint of disappointment before she covers it up with a smile. "Yeah, of course. Go do your CEO thing."

I hesitate, not wanting to leave things like this. "Don't disappear on me, okay? I'll find you later." I reach my hand out, letting it slide gently around her waist. "I'm sorry I have to step away again."

She gives me a small smile, and there's a softness in her eyes that gives me hope. "I'll be around."

I need to kiss her, to taste her but I can't be rushed. Not the first time. I need to be able to savor her, to take my time. I let my hand fall from her body with a small nod.

As I walk away, I can't help but glance back at her, the glow of the Christmas tree lights reflecting off her skin, making her look almost ethereal. My chest tightens, and I realize just how much I don't want this night to end. For the first time in a while, I feel like I'm not just playing a part, but like I've found something real, something that's not just about business deals or impressing people.

I take a deep breath, forcing myself to focus on the task at hand, but as I shake hands and nod through the conversation with my associate, my mind keeps drifting back to Ivy. The way she looked at me, the way she talked about baking and life, the way she made me feel like maybe—just maybe—there's more to this holiday party than networking and putting on a show.

When I finally manage to wrap things up, I scan the room, hoping to catch a glimpse of her dark hair or the sparkle of her dress. But I don't see her. The conversation took longer than expected and I glance down at my watch.

"Shit." It's just after midnight already. I feel my pocket buzz and pull out my phone to see a text from Ivy.

IVY

> Sorry I left without saying goodbye! Feet were killing me. Let me know when you're interested in your next chemistry lesson. 😉

The smile that's been plastered on my face all night because of her returns. I almost type out a quick response but decide to hold off, waiting to craft the perfect response when I can offer her a time to hang out.

"What's with that look?" Zane mutters as he shuffles over to me.

"What are you still doing here? I'm shocked you stuck around after the first hour."

He shrugs, his bow tie hanging loose around his neck, an almost finished cocktail in his hand. "Open bar got me," he says, raising his glass.

The look on his face tells me that is not the reason he stuck around tonight—or at least not the only reason. I'm about to ask who she is but I decide I'm too wrapped up in my head right now to hear about his latest conquest.

"Well, I'm beat, think I'm gonna head out. You good?" he asks, grabbing my shoulder.

"Great," I assure him, grabbing my now warm champagne flute and lifting it toward his glass. "To another successful holiday party in the books."

I don't know what's going to happen next with Ivy and me, but I do know one thing—whatever it is, I don't want to miss it.

Because for the first time in a long time, I feel like I'm exactly where I'm supposed to be. And I'm not about to let that slip away.

CHAPTER 7
IVY

"Thanks for inviting me to join you for your first time." My eyes squeeze shut for a second. *Shit.* "I mean your first time at the Christmas market," I quickly correct and he doesn't even attempt to hide his laugh, the tension that's been evident since we reconnected growing thick.

The wind is brisk as we step into the bustling holiday market, our breaths forming little clouds in the chilly air. Snowflakes swirl around us, dusting the rows of market stalls with a soft layer of white. The air is filled with the cozy, inviting scents of roasted chestnuts, spiced cider, and freshly baked gingerbread. Lights twinkle on every garland-draped stall, casting a warm glow over the bustling crowds. Asher walks beside me, his hands tucked into the pockets of his coat, a wool scarf wrapped around his neck. He looks like the kind of guy you'd see in one of those Hallmark movies Tessa loves.

"This is amazing," he says, glancing around with a boyish grin that makes my chest feel strangely light. He gestures toward the festive scene with a tilt of his head. "I've lived in Chicago my entire life, but I've never done this. Thanks for coming with me."

I smile, catching a snowflake on my glove and brushing it away.

"I can't believe you've never been to the Christmas market. It's one of the best parts of the season. It's practically a Chicago institution."

He gives a sheepish shrug, the grin never leaving his face. "Guess I've been too busy playing the part of the serious CEO. I don't usually take the time for this kind of thing."

"Well, you've been missing out," I say, giving him a teasing nudge with my shoulder. "Maybe this is your chance to catch up."

His gaze lingers on me for a beat longer than I expect, something warm and unguarded in his eyes. "Maybe it is."

We wander deeper into the market, sipping hot chocolate from steaming mugs that warm our hands. The sweetness mingles with the coolness of the air, and I find myself relaxing more with every step. We pass by stalls selling handmade ornaments, knitted scarves, and brightly painted nutcrackers. A vendor calls out, offering samples of warm cider, and Asher accepts a cup, his smile widening as he takes a sip.

"This is actually really good," he says, holding up the cup in a mock toast. "You weren't kidding about the market. I'm starting to feel like I've been doing Christmas all wrong."

I laugh, the sound mingling with the festive music playing from a nearby stall. "You probably have. But I'm here to help you fix that. And it starts with this." I point to a stall overflowing with handmade ornaments and snow globes, each one glistening under the fairy lights. "You can't visit the Christmas market without picking out an ornament."

Asher raises an eyebrow, following my gaze to the display. "Is that a rule?"

"It's practically law," I say, trying to keep a straight face. "And trust me, you do not want to be on Santa's naughty list for breaking it."

"Hmm—I dunno, the naughty list can be pretty fun." He inches a centimeter closer, his eyes dropping down to my lips.

"Are you trying to be a bad influence on me, Asher?" I raise my eyebrow. "I thought you were the good boy out of the two Mercers."

He chuckles, shaking his head as he steps up to the stall and picks up a small wooden snowflake, turning it over in his hands. The intricate carvings catch the light, casting delicate shadows. He holds it out toward me, a playful smile tugging at his lips. "What do you think? Does this meet your high standards for holiday cheer?"

I reach out, brushing my fingers against the smooth wood. "It's beautiful," I say honestly, glancing up at him. "You have good taste."

He looks back at me, something almost teasing in his expression. "Was that a compliment? From Ivy Calloway?"

I roll my eyes, but I can't stop the smile spreading across my face. "Don't get used to it."

He laughs, slipping the ornament back onto the display with a deliberate slowness, as if savoring the moment. "I'll try not to let it go to my head."

We continue walking through the market, moving from stall to stall, the snow falling gently around us. The lights shimmer on the fresh snowflakes that land on Asher's hair, and I feel a strange sense of calm settle over me—like maybe, for once, I don't have to think so hard about every word I say or every glance I steal.

Asher stops at a stall selling hand-carved wooden toys, his gaze lingering on a miniature sleigh. "You know, Zane and I used to have a sleigh like this when we were kids. We'd race it down the hill behind our house until we nearly broke our necks."

I laugh at the mental image. "I remember that hill. It was practically a death trap when it iced over."

He grins, leaning a little closer as if sharing a secret. "Yeah, well, we thought we were invincible back then. Zane crashed the sleigh into a tree once and split the thing in half. My dad was furious, but we just thought it made us look cooler."

I shake my head, smiling. "That sounds like you. Always pushing the limits, even when it made absolutely no sense."

He shrugs, a self-deprecating smile tugging at his lips. "What can I say? Guess I haven't changed much."

I glance at him, and for a moment, I see past the confident exterior he wears so well—past the smile, the charm, the easy way he commands a room. There's something softer there, something he doesn't show many people, and it makes me want to know more. I tilt my head, giving him a playful look. "Well, I'd like to think you've matured a little since then. At least enough to know not to challenge a tree to a duel."

Asher laughs, and the sound is warm and genuine, like a crackling fire on a cold night. "I promise, no more tree duels. I've learned my lesson."

We move on to another stall, this one selling delicate glass ornaments. Asher picks up a tiny snow globe with a miniature Christmas village inside, the little houses dusted with fake snow. He gives it a gentle shake, watching the snow swirl around the scene inside.

"You know," he says, turning the snow globe in his hands, "I never really understood the appeal of these things when I was younger. But now... there's something kind of magical about them. Like a whole world in your hands."

I smile softly, feeling a little pang of nostalgia. "I used to collect them. When I was a kid, I had a whole shelf full of snow globes from every place my family traveled. I liked the idea that I could capture a little piece of a place and keep it with me."

He looks at me, something curious in his expression. "Do you still have them?"

I shake my head, a little wistful. "I lost most of them when my parents moved to a different neighborhood a few years ago. But I've started a new collection. One snow globe every year, from somewhere special."

His eyes brighten, and he holds the snow globe out toward me. "Then I think you should add this one to your collection. A souvenir from tonight."

I take the snow globe from him, feeling a warm flutter in my chest. "Are you sure? It's your first time here—you should keep it."

He shakes his head, his smile turning gentle. "It's a memory I'd rather share with you." He holds his card out to the woman behind the stall, purchasing the globe.

For a second, I'm speechless, caught off guard by the sincerity in his voice. I look down at the snow globe in my hands, at the little village inside, and then back up at him. "Thank you, Asher. Really."

He shrugs, trying to play it off, but I can see the faint pink tinge on his cheeks, and it makes something inside me soften. "It's just a snow globe, Ivy. No big deal."

"Maybe not to you," I reply, a smile tugging at my lips, "but to me, it's kind of perfect."

He holds my gaze for a beat longer, then glances away, clearing his throat. "So, what's next on the holiday tour? Should we find some roasted chestnuts or try out that skating rink over there?" He points to a rink just beyond the market stalls, where couples and families glide across the ice under the glow of fairy lights.

I follow his gaze, feeling a flicker of excitement. "Only if you're ready to risk bruising your pride. I'm pretty good on skates, you know."

He gives me a mock-serious look, raising an eyebrow. "Is that a challenge?"

"Absolutely," I reply, stepping closer to him, our shoulders nearly brushing. "Unless you're afraid of being shown up. Maybe there's something you're not amazing at—"

He leans in, lowering his voice as a playful grin spreads across his face. "Ivy Calloway, you have a little snark to you, you know that? I think you're starting to enjoy this—challenging me."

I tilt my head, meeting his gaze without flinching. "Maybe I am."

The words slip out before I can second-guess them, and for a moment, the world seems to pause. His smile softens, turning almost contemplative, and the look in his eyes makes my heart race. He opens his mouth, like he's about to say something more, but then a gust of wind sends a swirl of snowflakes dancing around us, and the spell is broken.

"Well, come on, then," he says, holding out a hand with an exaggerated flourish. "Show me what you've got."

I hesitate for only a second before slipping my gloved hand into his, letting him lead me toward the skating rink. The contact is brief, but it leaves my skin tingling, my mind buzzing with the possibilities of what might come next.

We lace up our skates, the cold biting at our noses and cheeks, but I hardly feel it. I'm too focused on the way Asher's smile keeps slipping into something softer when he looks at me, like he's seeing me in a new light. As we step onto the ice, he wobbles a bit, catching himself with a laugh that echoes through the night air.

"Don't worry, I won't let you fall," I tease, skating a circle around him with ease.

He narrows his eyes at me, a playful challenge in his expression. "Is that so? We'll see about that."

I laugh, pushing off to glide across the ice, and he follows, a little unsteady but determined. For a while, we just skate, weaving in and out of the other skaters, the lights above us casting shadows that stretch and shimmer on the ice. He picks up speed, closing the distance between us, and I can't help the rush of exhilaration that courses through me.

Asher catches up to me, his breath visible in the cold air, and he reaches out, gently tugging on the end of my scarf. "You're a show-off, you know that?"

I grin, turning to skate backward so I can face him. "Hey, I told you I was good. You should've believed me."

He laughs, a sound that sends warmth blooming in my chest. "Okay, okay, I believe you. But I think you owe me a little mercy."

I slow down, letting him catch his breath, and he comes to a stop beside me, still gripping the end of my scarf. For a moment, we just stand there, our breaths mingling in the frosty air, the lights casting a golden halo around us.

"I'm really glad we did this, Ivy," he says quietly, his voice carrying a hint of something deeper. "I feel like... I'm seeing a whole new side of you tonight."

I swallow, feeling a lump rise in my throat. It's terrifying, being this close to someone, letting them see the parts of you you've kept hidden for so long. But when I look into Asher's eyes, I see something genuine there, something that makes me want to take the risk.

"Maybe you are," I say softly, my voice barely more than a whisper, "but I'm still the same girl who likes mystery novels and dragons."

He smiles, stepping closer, his hand brushing mine. "And I like that girl. A lot."

My breath catches, and for a moment, I think he might kiss me. But instead, he just holds my gaze, his thumb tracing a slow circle over the back of my hand. And even though the distance between us is maddening, I realize that maybe, for tonight, this is enough.

CHAPTER 8
ASHER

Wandering through the market with Ivy by my side after our skating adventure, I keep my steps slow, savoring the moment. The festive buzz is fading as we near the last few rows of stalls, the snow falling like a perfect white veil over everything. She's right there, so close that her warmth radiates through the cold air. I don't even feel the chill nipping at my skin. Honestly, nothing feels cold when Ivy's next to me.

We reach the end of the market, where evergreen trees wrapped in twinkling lights frame a picture-perfect scene. But it's not the trees that catch my eye. It's the mistletoe swaying between two of them, almost like it's begging for attention. I can't help the slow grin spreading across my face.

"Well, look at that," I murmur, my voice low and playful as I nod toward the mistletoe. "Seems like we've found ourselves in a bit of a situation."

Ivy's gaze follows mine, and when she spots the mistletoe, her laugh comes out nervous, but cute as hell. "It's just a silly tradition," she says, trying to play it cool, but I don't miss the flicker of excitement in her eyes. Her pulse is practically racing, and I can feel the tension in the air between us.

God, I love this. The tension, the anticipation, the delicious temptation of leaning forward and pulling her into my arms as my tongue explores her mouth.

"Is it?" I take a step closer, letting the snow crunch under my boots as the space between us shrinks. Her breath is warm against the winter chill, and I can't stop looking at her lips. So close, but not quite touching. "Or maybe," I add, voice dropping just enough to send a shiver through her, "it's an opportunity."

She swallows, and I catch the sound in the quiet night, the way her breath hitches just a little. That's when I know I have her attention. Her eyes dart to mine, and there's a challenge there, a spark that makes my heart pound harder.

"Asher..." Her voice wavers, but I hear the unspoken question in it. I step in even closer, until the heat between us makes the world around us blur. The snow, the market, everything just fades away.

"What?" I ask, my tone soft, teasing, but there's a flicker of seriousness beneath it. "Too much of a cliché for you? We could just walk away, pretend we didn't see it."

I'm daring her now, testing her boundaries, and I feel a moment of uncertainty myself. Ivy Calloway, the woman who seems to have everything together—what if I'm reading this wrong? But the way she looks at me, the way her lips part ever so slightly, tells me I'm right where I need to be.

"It's not that," she whispers, her voice barely audible, "it's just..."

I lean in, just enough that our noses brush, that electricity sparking between us. "What are you afraid of, Ivy?" My voice is low, coaxing. I want her to say it. To admit what we're both feeling.

Her eyes meet mine, and for a second, I feel the weight of the world holding its breath. It's just her and me, standing beneath the mistletoe, caught in something we both know isn't just about a silly holiday tradition.

"I'm afraid that if I kiss you," she says, her voice soft but full of honesty, "I won't want it to be just a silly tradition."

Her words slam into me, and for a second, I freeze. Did she really just say that? I can't help the smile that breaks across my face. A slow, genuine grin that has nothing to do with teasing. I reach up, brushing a snowflake from her hair, my fingers lingering a little longer than necessary.

"Maybe I don't want it to be just a tradition either," I reply, my voice barely louder than a whisper, as if I'm afraid to break the spell between us. "Maybe I'm hoping it's the start of something."

There's a shift in her, a softening that pulls me in even further. She looks up at me, and I can see the decision flickering in her eyes. Her hand moves up to touch my face, her glove brushing against my stubble, and it's like every nerve in my body is suddenly on high alert.

Time slows, the space between us humming with tension and unspoken words. And then she rises up on her toes, and before I can even think, her lips are on mine. Soft, tentative, like she's asking a question I've been dying to answer.

For a heartbeat, I'm frozen. Not because I don't want this—God, I've wanted this for so long—but because it feels too perfect. But then instinct kicks in, and I pull her closer, my hand slipping behind her neck, my fingers tangling in her hair as I kiss her back.

Really fucking kiss her.

My lips move against hers, slowly, gently for a few seconds before passion takes over. I slide my tongue between them, a soft moan slipping from her lips into my mouth. My cock stiffens against her, her body melting against me as I deepen the kiss, both of us completely lost in each other.

The world disappears. There's no snow, no market, no people milling around. Just Ivy, her lips warm against mine, her body pressed close as if she's been waiting for this as long as I have. The kiss deepens, and I feel her relax into me, a soft sound escaping her lips that makes my pulse race even harder.

I can't stop the smile that forms as I pull her even closer, the warmth of her mouth a perfect contrast to the cold around us. When we finally break apart, both of us breathless, our foreheads resting together, I take a moment to just enjoy it. Snowflakes are melting against our skin, but I don't care. All I can think about is the way she kissed me like she meant it, like she wanted more just like me.

"Fuck," I murmur, my voice rougher than I expect. "That was…" I lean in again, taking another minute to enjoy her lips again. "Sorry," I whisper when I pull back, "I need to stop."

She laughs softly, the sound reminding me that we're still in public and despite what I want, I can't take things further.

"I didn't ask you to stop."

I reach out, brushing my thumb over her bottom lip, feeling the way she shivers under my touch. "Mmm, don't say that…" The tension ratchets back up, both of us leaning in again, our bodies doing all the talking.

When I pull back from her this time, I put physical distance between us, stepping back and sucking in a deep breath, groaning when I let it out. I reach down, attempting to adjust my rigid cock that's begging for even a second of relief.

"Goddamn." I laugh, Ivy's eyes dropping down to the evidence, her cheeks flushing again. "You really know how to test a man's limits."

"I'm sure you've suffered worse," she teases, her hands reaching out to rest softly against my chest as she looks up at me.

"For a scientist, you're damn good at breaking the laws of chemistry."

Her eyes spark with amusement as she raises an eyebrow at my corny attempt at a joke. "What can I say? Sometimes, you have to defy the rules to make something truly spectacular."

I lean in, my lips barely brushing hers again. "I think you might be the most intriguing person I've ever met, Ivy Calloway."

"Careful, Asher," she whispers, her breath mingling with mine, "you keep saying things like that, and I might start to believe you."

I smile, pressing a gentle kiss to her forehead, my mind wondering if there's something more behind that comment, like maybe she's worried this is all I'm after—but that couldn't be further from the truth.

"Maybe I want you to believe it."

For a moment, we just stand there, holding each other beneath the mistletoe. The world could fall apart around us, and I don't think I'd notice. All I feel is her warmth, the steady rhythm of her breath matching mine, and the quiet certainty that I don't want to let this moment slip away.

It's weird. We are strangers, there's no way around it, even if we have a past. We didn't know one another in high school and we still don't truly know each other but there's something between us that feels deeper than any connection I've ever had, like there's always been something pulling us back to each other.

When she finally looks up at me, her smile is small, unsure. "So, what now? Do we just pretend this didn't happen?"

I shake my head, my voice steady. "No. I don't want to pretend. I don't know what this is yet, but I know I don't want it to be a one-time thing."

Her expression softens, and I see the hope in her eyes. "I don't know what this is either," she admits, "but I think... I think I'd like to find out."

I grin, kissing her forehead again before pulling back slightly, my hands still resting on her waist. "Good. Because I'm not letting you go just yet."

She laughs, her breath warm against the cold. "You better not, Asher Mercer." She clutches my coat in her gloved hands, her walls slowly coming down more and more, letting me see what's really behind those dark, mysterious eyes. "Because if you do, I might just find a way to turn you into a cookie recipe."

I laugh, leaning down to kiss her quickly. "She's feisty. I like it."

"You have no idea," she teases, biting my lip gently.

"Just promise you won't burn the edges."

She looks at me, her eyes full of something soft, something real, like she sees past the false bravado I put on. Past the CEO, past the smile and charm. She sees me.

Ivy's laugh is light and full of warmth, the kind that sinks into your chest and settles there, burrowing deep. "No promises," she teases, her voice soft as she steps back, just enough to put some space between us, though her fingers linger against mine. The market has mostly emptied out, but neither of us seems eager to go back to wherever we were headed before this moment.

I let my thumb glide over the back of her hand, enjoying the quiet simplicity of just standing there with her. But there's something else in the air now—a buzz, a tension that hasn't quite left us since that kiss under the mistletoe. I feel like I should say something, anything to keep her close for a little longer. My place isn't far, and the thought of going back to an empty apartment, when I could be with her instead, feels... wrong.

"Do you want to head back to my place?" I ask, the words coming out more casually than I expected, but there's an edge of anticipation in my tone. "It's not far, and I've got some hot chocolate... if that sounds like your kind of after-market drink."

"Oh, the old 'my place isn't far' cliché, huh?" She giggles.

I grin, stepping closer again, catching her scent, a mix of that sweet vanilla and something uniquely hers. "Yeah, but sometimes clichés are just... comfortable. Or maybe I'm just hoping to spend a little more time with you." My tone drops lower, the flirtation obvious now, and I'm rewarded with the slight flush that spreads across her cheeks.

I lean in, close enough that our noses almost brush, my voice a low murmur. "I make it with real chocolate. No powder mix in sight. I think you'll be impressed."

She rolls her eyes playfully but laughs. "Alright, you've convinced me."

With a lingering smile, I take her hand, threading my fingers through hers, and together, we walk out of the market. The snow falls more steadily now, blanketing the street in a quiet kind of calm as we head toward my place, our steps in sync.

My apartment is modest compared to most millionaires—wood floors, a couple of bookshelves, a fireplace in the corner that I rarely use. It's not elaborate and it doesn't really feel much like a home but right now, with her here, it feels like everything. I toss my keys onto the small table near the door and flick on a few lights, giving the space a soft glow.

"Wow." She glances around. "Your place is so cozy, so— masculine."

I give her a playful grin as I walk toward the kitchen. "Cozy, huh? I'll take that as a compliment." I pause, turning to catch her eye again. "So, you want that hot chocolate?"

"You weren't kidding," she says, leaning on the counter, watching me with an amused smile. "I'm starting to think you planned this."

Her cheeks flush again, and I can't help but let my gaze linger on her lips, remembering how they felt pressed against mine. The silence between us hums with tension. When I finish the drinks, I slide one over to her, letting my fingers brush hers deliberately. The spark that flares between us isn't just in my head; I know she feels it too.

She takes a sip, closing her eyes for a moment as the warmth of the chocolate hits her. "Okay, I'll admit it. This is really good."

"You know," I murmur, my voice low and rough with the weight of everything I'm feeling. "I can't stop thinking about that kiss," I admit, knowing I'm pushing my luck.

Her breath hitches, and her eyes darken just a bit, her lips parting. "Me either."

That's all the permission I need. In one smooth motion, I close the distance between us, my mouth capturing hers again, but this time, there's no hesitation. I pull her flush against me, deepening the kiss as my hands move up her back, drawing her closer until there's nothing between us but the heat that's been building all night.

Ivy responds instantly, her fingers sliding into my hair, tugging just enough to send a spark of heat shooting down my spine. Her lips move against mine, confident now, as if we've both been holding back since we left the market, and now that it's here, we're not holding back. The kiss turns hungry, the tension snapping like a rubber band that's been pulled too tight for too long.

When we finally break apart, we're both breathless, her hands still tangled in my hair, my arms wrapped tightly around her. Our foreheads rest against each other, the air between us thick with something undeniable.

"This," I whisper, my voice husky with desire, "feels like a lot more than just a silly tradition."

She smiles, a slow, wicked smile that makes my pulse quicken. "You're right about that."

Without another word, I lift her onto the counter, stepping between her legs as I lean in for another kiss, harder this time, more certain. The tension that's been building between us all night finally breaks, and I know that whatever this is, it's just the beginning.

Ivy's hands tighten in my hair, her body pressing against my cock. The kiss deepens, the rhythm of it changing, no longer tentative but filled with a kind of urgency that matches the pulse in my chest. I grip her waist, feeling the warmth of her body seeping through my fingers as I pull her even closer. Her hips move slightly against me, her body begging for some friction between her thighs.

She lets out a soft, breathy sound that drives me wild, and I can't help but slip my hands up under her sweater, feeling the soft skin beneath. Her breath hitches at the touch, and when she pulls back to look at me, her eyes are dark, her pupils wide with desire. There's something raw between us now, like we've both stopped pretending this was just a casual evening.

I lean in again, pressing a kiss to the corner of her mouth, trailing down the side of her neck, feeling her pulse quicken under my lips. She tilts her head back, giving me more access, her hands sliding down to grip my shoulders, anchoring herself as she shivers from my touch. I can feel the heat rising between us, the kind of heat that makes me forget about everything else—the cold, the snow, the world outside.

I pull back just enough to look at her, my hands resting on her hips as I catch my breath. "Ivy," I murmur, "if you don't want me to strip you naked and spend the next several hours tasting every fucking inch of you, you need to tell me no right now. You understand me?"

Her eyes search mine, and for a second, I see the flicker of uncertainty, but it fades just as quickly as it came. Her answer is clear in the way her hands tighten around me, pulling me closer.

"Yes," she whispers, her voice steady despite the shaky breath that follows. "Take me, Asher."

That's all I need. My lips crash against hers again, more urgent this time, more intense. Her hands roam over my chest, then down, tugging at my shirt as if she's just as desperate for more as I am. I don't hesitate, lifting her off the counter and carrying her toward the couch. Her laughter fills the space between kisses, a light sound that only fuels the fire.

I set her down gently, then join her on the couch, leaning over her as my hands find her waist again. Ivy pulls me down on top of her, her lips never leaving mine as she shifts beneath me, her legs tangling with mine. The kiss becomes more heated, more demanding, and I can feel the last traces of control slipping away as I lose myself in her.

"I need a taste," I say between kisses as I trail my lips down her neck, lifting her sweater up and over her head in a rush.

Her laughter is gone, along with any trace of the lighthearted conversation from earlier. Her body arches beneath me, her hands in my hair as I slide her skirt up her thighs, running my nose and lips against the tights she's wearing. My fingers reach the waistband of them and her panties and I instantly pull them down, tossing them to the side.

She intakes a sharp breath when my fingers touch her bare skin, gliding up gently as I press her thighs apart.

"Let me taste you," I say gently, leaning in, my mouth already watering at the sight of her pink, glistening pussy that's begging for my tongue to swipe right up the center.

"Ohhh." Her moan is deeper, her thighs spreading on their own, her hands tightening in my hair as I take my time swirling, tasting, and savoring every drop of her.

"Asher." My name comes out as a cry when her orgasm reaches her. She pants, moaning and writhing against my tongue in a way that will be burned into my brain. Her flavor sends a possessive jolt through me, like her flavor was made for me.

But there's something else in this, too. It's not just the desire, though that's impossible to ignore; it's the way her touch feels like it's lighting me up from the inside, like every kiss, every glance is stoking something deeper. Something I didn't realize I'd been waiting for.

When I finally climb back over her, I wrap my hand around her jaw, holding her steady while I dip my tongue into her mouth, making her taste her release on my tongue. I break the kiss, my forehead resting against hers as we both catch our breath, her chest rising and falling rapidly beneath me. Her eyes flutter open, and when she meets my gaze, there's no hesitation left in them. Just her, fully in this moment with me.

"More, I need more." Her hands are on my belt, undoing it followed by my zipper.

"You're sure?" I ask, my voice low, rough with need but tinged with the last thread of restraint I'm holding on to.

She nods, her fingers tracing the line of my jaw with one hand, her other sliding beneath my waistband and wrapping tightly around my cock, making me groan.

"I've never been more sure of anything."

Those words hit me like a shot of adrenaline, and I lean down to kiss her again, softer this time, savoring the way she melts into it. I can feel her hands roaming over me, pulling me closer, and I'm lost in the sensation of her—of her warmth.

"Then I hope you're ready to take me over." I reach down, freeing my cock and lining it up at her entrance. "And over." I press the tip against her warmth, her pussy stretching to accommodate my girth.

"If I can." Her breath hitches, her thighs squeezing my ribs tightly as she lets out a shaky breath.

"Oh, we'll work you up to it." My voice sounds like I've been drinking all night, my throat tightening as I hold back from pressing all the way inside her. "That's right, Ivy." I guide myself in and out of her in small increments. "See how wet your pussy is getting for me. Just relax and let me show you how to take my cock, baby girl."

Our fingers are intertwined, both of her hands pinned above her head as I pump in and out of her, my strokes long and slow. I lean down, pulling her bra down with my teeth, wrapping my lips around her nipple.

Her eyes are struggling to stay on mine, rolling back into her head as her back arches, her hips lifting to meet my strokes.

"Look at you fucking me back." I try to keep my composure but I'm hanging by a thread. Her jaw clenches, her head lulling back so her neck is exposed to my lips. I take advantage just as I feel her walls clench around me, milking me for every last drop as she joins me in my release, crying out, her own orgasm tearing through her body.

I LEAN BACK IN MY CHAIR, THE CREAK OF LEATHER BENEATH ME PUNCTUATING the otherwise quiet office, and my gaze drifts out the window to the snow-covered skyline. Chicago looks peaceful under its thick layer of snow, but my thoughts are far from tranquil. They're tangled up in memories of last night—memories of Ivy.

My pulse quickens, my dick sore but ready for another night of marathon sex.

My phone buzzes on the desk, and I can't help the grin that tugs at the corner of my lips when I see her name flash across the screen.

IVY

You end up making it into the office?

IVY

Or are you just daydreaming about me at home?

I bite back a chuckle. That woman knows how to keep me on my toes, even through text.

ME

You caught me. I'm staring out the window, trying to figure out how to focus after last night.

ME

You do have a way of leaving a lasting impression, Calloway.

My thumb hovers over the send button, a thousand things I'd rather be saying than texting her. Things like how her skin felt under my hands, how the memory of her lips still lingers like a fire I can't put out. Hell, how I'm struggling to keep my mind on anything but her.

Her response comes quickly.

IVY

Mmm, do I?

IVY

I guess that's what happens when you combine great company with a little holiday… magic. 😉

That little winking face does something to me—something that makes it impossible to focus on the reports sitting on my desk. I shift in my chair, memories flooding back in vivid detail. The feel of her warm body against mine, the way her breath caught when my hands roamed her curves. The way she whispered my name, making it sound like something sacred.

My phone buzzes again, pulling me from the vivid memory.

IVY

Or maybe you're just terrible at focusing.

I laugh out loud this time, running a hand through my hair. She's not wrong.

ME

I think you're the problem, not my focus. I'm usually much better at handling distractions.

ME

But you... you're a distraction I'm willing to make time for. A distraction I hope wants to stick around.

There's a pause on her end, and I can almost picture her biting her lip as she reads my reply, her cheeks flushed from whatever smart retort she's about to send.

IVY

Good to know I have such an effect on the infamous Asher Mercer. I guess I'll have to take full advantage of that.

Her words linger in my mind, the innuendo clear. My body tightens at the thought of "full advantage," and I find myself shifting again in my chair, trying to get comfortable. This woman has no idea what she's doing to me—or maybe she does, and that's exactly the problem.

My assistant's voice crackles through the intercom, pulling me back into the moment. "Mr. Mercer, your meeting with the marketing team is in fifteen minutes."

I reply with a quick, "Thanks, Keri," but my head is still full of Ivy

—how she felt beneath me, how her eyes had softened as she traced lazy patterns on my chest afterward, her lips swollen from our kisses. The way her body felt so natural against mine. Suddenly a pang of regret hits my ribs.

Why didn't I make an effort in high school? We could be ten years in the future right now.

I glance down at my phone, hesitating before sending one more message, my thumb moving across the screen deliberately.

ME

I can't stop thinking about last night.

ME

You're dangerous, Ivy Calloway. You've got me thinking about things I shouldn't be thinking about while I'm sitting in my office. Making me wish you were spread out on my desk right now so I could take my lunch early.

There. Let her chew on that while I try to get through this meeting without completely losing my head.

I don't even bother to look up when I hear a knock at the door. Zane's unmistakable presence fills the room as he steps in, leaning against the doorframe with that same damn smirk he always wears when he's about to get on my case.

"I know, I know, I'm late for the marketing meeting."

"You've been staring out that window for a good twenty minutes. Want to tell me what's going on, little brother?" His eyes gleam with amusement, and it doesn't take a genius to figure out what—or who—he thinks is responsible for my distraction.

I shrug, trying to play it cool, but there's no hiding the fact that Ivy's still on my mind. "Just thinking about some things," I say, leaning back in my chair, trying to suppress the grin that threatens to spread, "nothing important."

Zane raises an eyebrow, stepping inside and closing the door behind him with a soft click. "Yeah, right. I heard you've been spending time with Ivy Calloway. Interesting choice, Asher. She's not like the usual girls you entertain."

The way he says "entertain" makes my jaw clench. Zane has always had a knack for seeing through me. I shoot him a look, trying to keep things casual. "I'm working with her and Tessa on that new business. I'm just giving them some advice."

He snorts. "Advice, huh? And that's why you took her to the Christmas market? And why you look like you're seconds away from spacing out again right now and clearly didn't get an ounce of sleep last night."

I can't help but shift in my chair, the taste of Ivy—of her skin, her lips, her breathless moans—still fresh on my tongue and lips. "It's... not what you think," I lie, but even I don't believe it.

Zane arches an eyebrow, his skeptical expression cutting right through me. "Sure, it's not. Look, I get it. Ivy's smart, driven, not like the usual women you've been involved with. But that's exactly why you need to tread carefully."

I roll my eyes, leaning forward and resting my elbows on the desk. "Why do you care, Zane? Since when do you care about who I spend time with?"

His expression softens, and for a moment, I see that brotherly concern in his eyes, something I don't see often. "Because I know how you get when someone catches your interest. You dive in, you play with fire, and when it burns out, you walk away without looking back."

I narrow my eyes at him, even though I know he's right. I've never let anyone get close enough to burn me. But Ivy? She's different. She's already so far under my skin, I don't know if I could walk away even if I wanted to.

"I'm not trying to screw anything up," I mutter, more to myself than to him. "She's not like anyone else."

Zane looks at me for a long moment, then sighs, standing up and patting my shoulder. "Just be careful, Asher. Don't drag her into your world if you're not ready for what comes with that."

As he heads for the door, my phone buzzes again. I glance down, my heart skipping a beat when I see Ivy's reply.

IVY

I can't stop thinking about last night either.

IVY

Maybe we should do something about that. Tonight?

A slow smile spreads across my face as I type my reply.

ME

You're on. My place at eight.

I lean back, that tension in my chest loosening a little. For the first time in a long time, I'm not interested in running. Not from her. Ivy's got me hooked—and tonight, I plan on showing her just how deep that hook goes.

The excitement bubbling in my chest makes it hard to focus on anything else. My stomach is doing somersaults, and my heart feels like it's trying to race out of my chest as I move around my apartment. I'm going to see Asher again tonight. It's silly how giddy I feel, like a teenager getting ready for a date, but I can't help it. I've replayed last night in my head so many times, it's become almost like a movie reel.

I close my eyes for a moment, leaning against the counter. His hands, the warmth of his touch, the way he looked at me like I was the only person in the world. I smile to myself, feeling the heat rise to my cheeks just thinking about how everything between us felt so easy, so right. Tonight, I'll be back at his place, and the anticipation makes me feel like I'm floating on air.

But the excitement is threaded with a touch of anxiety, the nagging voice in the back of my head that wonders if maybe last time was just a fluke, something magical that won't last in the harsh light of day.

What if tonight feels different? What if I'm overthinking all of this?

I glance at the clock. I still have a couple of hours before I'm supposed to head over, so I grab my apron and decide to bake. It's one of the few things that calms my nerves and helps me focus when my thoughts start to spiral. Plus, Asher said he loves gingerbread, so maybe I can surprise him with a batch.

I pull out the ingredients, and before long, the sweet, spicy scent of gingerbread fills the kitchen. Mixing the dough, cutting out the shapes, and carefully placing them on the baking sheet helps to settle my jittery energy. But no matter how much I try to distract myself, my mind keeps wandering back to him. To us.

This morning, when I left his place, we didn't make any promises or declarations. There was no awkwardness, just a quiet understanding that whatever this was between us, it wasn't over. And tonight, I'd be stepping back into his world—his sleek, polished world that feels so different from mine, but that somehow made me feel like I belonged, at least for those moments with him.

I peek into the oven, the golden edges of the cookies just starting to crisp. They're turning out perfectly. My phone buzzes on the counter, and my heart skips a beat when I see his name.

> ASHER
>
> Can't wait to see you tonight. Miss you already.

My cheeks flush, and I bite my lip, feeling that giddy warmth spread through me again. It's hard to believe that this is the same man who always seemed so untouchable—this larger-than-life figure who somehow made me feel like I was the only one who mattered when we were together.

> ME
>
> I'm bringing a surprise, so I hope you're ready.

I add a little winking emoji, feeling playful. It's strange how easily I've fallen into this rhythm with him, teasing, flirting—it feels like a game, one I'm more than happy to play.

I finish up the baking and pack the gingerbread cookies into a small tin, wrapping it with a festive bow. It's not much, but I know Asher will appreciate the effort. My excitement builds again as I get ready, slipping into something casual but nice—a sweater dress and some black thigh boots. It's nothing too fancy, but it's comfortable and feels like me. A step up from my usual jeans, plus it hugs my hips and paired with the boots, it gives me a confidence boost.

Before long, I'm out the door, the tin of cookies tucked under my arm as I make my way to Asher's place. The snow has started to fall again, big, soft flakes that drift down slowly, coating the city in a pristine layer of white. The air is cold, but my heart feels warm, filled with the anticipation of seeing him again.

As I approach his building, my nerves return, but in the best way —the kind of fluttering excitement that comes when you're about to step into something you've been waiting for. I buzz up, and almost immediately, Asher's deep, familiar voice comes through the intercom.

"Hey, Ivy. Come on up."

The door buzzes open, and I step inside, my pulse quickening. The elevator ride feels like it takes forever, and I take a deep breath, reminding myself to just be me.

When the doors slide open and I step out, Asher is already waiting for me. He leans casually against the doorway of his apartment, looking effortlessly handsome in a black sweater and jeans. His face breaks into a slow, warm smile the moment he sees me, and my heart stumbles over itself.

"You're a sight for sore eyes," he says, his voice low and full of that teasing charm that makes my stomach do flips.

"I could say the same about you," I reply, trying to keep my cool, though my insides are practically vibrating with excitement.

He steps forward, reaching for the tin in my hands. "Is this my surprise?"

"Maybe," I say with a grin. "You'll have to open it and see."

He takes the tin from me, his fingers brushing against mine as he does, sending a warm shiver through me. His eyes linger on mine for just a moment longer than necessary before he opens the tin and inhales deeply. "Gingerbread. I love gingerbread."

"I remember," I say, feeling pleased with myself.

He reaches out and takes my hand, pulling me gently into the apartment. "You didn't have to do this, you know," he says, setting the tin down on the counter, "but I'm glad you did."

There's a softness in his voice that makes my heart swell, and before I can stop myself, I step closer, wrapping my arms around his waist. He doesn't hesitate—his arms slide around me, pulling me tight against him, and for a moment, we just stand there, holding each other.

"I missed you," I whisper against his chest, the words slipping out before I can think twice.

"I missed you too," he replies, his lips brushing the top of my head. He pulls back slightly, his hand coming up to tilt my chin so that I'm looking up at him. His gaze is intense, but there's something vulnerable in it, something that makes my heart beat faster. "I've been thinking about you... about us."

I nod, feeling that same vulnerability rising up in me, but I don't want to run from it. Not tonight. "Me too."

Asher's eyes flick down to my lips, and before I can say anything else, he leans in, capturing my mouth in a slow, deliberate kiss. It's gentle at first, almost hesitant, but when I respond, when I press into him, it deepens. His arms tighten around me, and I feel the tension between us start to melt away, replaced by that electric connection we've had since the beginning.

When we finally pull back, breathless, Asher rests his forehead against mine, his fingers lightly tracing the line of my jaw. "Ivy... I don't want this to just be a fling."

His words hang in the air between us, heavy and full of meaning.

My heart skips a beat, and I realize that I don't want that either. This, whatever this is, feels real. It feels right.

"Neither do I," I say softly, my voice steady, even though my heart is racing. "I'm not sure where this is going, but I want to find out."

He smiles, that genuine, heart-melting smile that makes me feel like maybe, just maybe, I've found something real.

"Good," he murmurs, pressing a kiss to my forehead, "because I'm not ready to let you go."

And just like that, the excitement and nervous energy I felt earlier fades, replaced by a quiet sense of certainty. This is the start of something new, something I didn't expect, but something I'm more than ready to dive into—cookies, nerves, and all.

The tension between us settles into something comfortable as Asher holds me close. His words—I'm not ready to let you go—echo in my mind, and I feel a flutter of hope in my chest. It feels surreal, like maybe the lines of reality and some perfect fantasy are blurring, but in the best way possible.

He releases me, but not entirely, his hand sliding down my arm until his fingers lightly hold mine. "Come on, let's sit down," he says softly, guiding me over to the couch. The room is lit softly, the glow of the fireplace giving everything a cozy, intimate feel. It's as if the rest of the world has disappeared, leaving just the two of us in this quiet, perfect bubble.

I settle onto the couch, my nerves easing the moment Asher sits next to me. He turns slightly, his knee brushing against mine, and I can feel the warmth of his presence radiating through the small space between us. It's like a magnetic pull, drawing us closer, even when we're already so close.

"So," he says, leaning back, a playful smile tugging at his lips, "tell me more about this surprise. Should I be flattered that you baked for me?"

I laugh, feeling a bit more at ease now, the anxiety that had been bubbling under the surface slowly fading. "You should be very flattered," I tease, nudging his knee with mine. "Not everyone gets special gingerbread cookies from me. Consider yourself lucky."

His eyes gleam with amusement. "Oh, I definitely do. Lucky and maybe a little spoiled." He leans in slightly, his voice dropping to a lower, more intimate tone. "I could get used to this."

The way he says it, with that flirtatious edge, sends a shiver down my spine. "Don't get too used to it," I reply, though my voice comes out softer, breathier than I expected. "I might have to keep you on your toes."

His grin widens, and he reaches out, tucking a loose strand of hair behind my ear. The touch is so simple, but it feels so intimate. "I like that idea," he murmurs, "but for the record, I'm happy to be spoiled by you."

The air between us shifts again, the playful flirting giving way to something deeper. His hand lingers near my face, his thumb brushing against my cheek, and I can feel my heart start to race. It's as if everything we've been skirting around—the attraction, the connection, the uncertainty—is crystallizing in this moment.

I don't want to break the spell, but I can't help the question that rises to my lips. "What are we doing, Asher?"

He doesn't pull away. If anything, he seems to lean in closer, his gaze steady and sincere as he searches my face. "I've been asking myself that same question," he admits softly, his fingers still gently tracing my skin. "I don't have all the answers. But I know that I don't want this to be casual. I don't want you to be just another part of my life that I drift away from."

His words sink in, making my heart swell with something that feels dangerously close to hope. "I don't want that either," I confess, my voice barely a whisper.

He exhales, like he's relieved to hear me say it, and then he cups my face with both hands, his expression more serious than I've ever seen it. "I know I can't promise everything will be easy. My life's... complicated. But I want to try. I want to figure this out with you, Ivy."

There's a sincerity in his voice that melts the last of my defenses. For so long, I've kept myself guarded, afraid of being hurt, afraid of letting someone in. But here he is, laying it all out there, offering me the very thing I've been too scared to admit I want.

"I want that too," I say, and the moment the words leave my mouth, I feel lighter, like a weight has been lifted off my shoulders. "I don't need everything figured out right now. I just want... this. You and me. Whatever this turns into."

He smiles then, the kind of smile that reaches his eyes, making them crinkle at the corners. "That sounds perfect to me."

Before I can say anything else, he pulls me closer, his lips finding mine in a slow, deliberate kiss. It's soft and sweet, needy and possessive all at once. I respond instantly, sinking into him, feeling the warmth of his body as his hands slip around my waist, holding me close.

We kiss like that for a while, unhurried and deep, each touch filled with a tenderness that makes my chest tighten. When we finally pull back, both of us breathless, I can't help the smile that tugs at my lips.

"What?" he asks, his own grin tugging at the corner of his mouth.

"Nothing," I murmur, shaking my head slightly, "it's just... I feel really happy right now. And I didn't think I'd be saying that."

His thumb brushes lightly over my lower lip, his gaze soft but intense. "I'm glad," he says quietly, leaning in to kiss me again, slower this time, like he's savoring the moment.

When we break apart, he pulls me against his chest, and I rest my head against him, feeling the steady rhythm of his heartbeat beneath my cheek. For a while, we sit like that, wrapped in each other, the soft glow of the fireplace casting shadows across the room.

I close my eyes, letting myself relax fully for the first time in what feels like forever. I don't know what tomorrow holds, but right now, in this moment, I'm content. I'm with him, and that's all that matters.

After a few minutes of comfortable silence, Asher's fingers start to play with my hair, his voice soft and playful as he says, "You know, if this gingerbread is as good as I think it'll be, you might have to come over and bake for me more often."

I laugh, rolling my eyes as I tilt my head up to look at him. "Oh, I see. This is all about getting more cookies out of me, isn't it?"

He grins, his hand still tangled in my hair as he leans down to kiss the tip of my nose. "Hey, I didn't say that. But if that's the perk of seeing you more, then I'm not complaining."

I shake my head, laughing softly as I snuggle back into him, feeling that familiar warmth spread through me again. "Well, I guess I can't deny a man his gingerbread cookies."

"Good," he says, his voice full of that playful charm again, "because I plan on keeping you around for a while. But right now..." He nips my lip. "I'm in the mood for a totally different kind of cookie."

The words are lighthearted, but there's something deeper behind them, something that makes my heart skip a beat. I squeeze his hand, feeling the weight of his promise, and for once, I let myself believe it. Believe that this—whatever it is—might be exactly what I've been waiting for.

"Yeah?" It's barely an audible word, his lips and tongue already doing things to me that have me feeling like I'm floating over my body in pure ecstasy.

I STRETCH, MY BODY SORE FROM ANOTHER NIGHT OF ASHER LEAVING ME completely spent and exhausted. The tinges of pain are delicious. I unbutton my shirt a little, pulling my bra down to see the purple outline of his teeth against my pale skin.

My body shivers and I glance at my phone again, half expecting another message from him, but nothing has come through yet. He dropped me off at home a couple of hours ago, giving me a sweet, lingering kiss at the door before heading out to deal with some work emergency. I could still feel the heat of his lips on mine and his lingering promise, "*I'll see you soon,*" echoing in my head.

The knock at the door pulls me from my thoughts, and I sit up, heart fluttering a little until I realize it's probably Tessa. She had texted earlier, saying she wanted to stop by after work to talk about the plans.

I pad over to the door and open it, finding Tessa grinning at me with two paper cups of coffee in hand. "Thought you might need a pick-me-up after the day you've had," she says, stepping inside and handing me a cup.

"You have no idea," I reply, accepting the cup gratefully. I close the door behind her and follow her back to the couch, where she promptly plops down and kicks off her shoes. I know she's been dying to ask me since I first told her Asher and I went to the Christmas market together.

"So," Tessa says, wiggling her eyebrows as she takes a sip of her coffee, "spill. How was it with Mr. CEO last night? Did he like the cookies?"

I laugh, shaking my head. "I knew you were going to start with that."

"Of course I am!" she says, her eyes sparkling with curiosity. "Don't leave me hanging! You've been all dreamy-eyed for days now."

I roll my eyes but can't stop the smile that creeps across my face. "Okay, fine. It was... really good. We talked about a lot of things, and, well... he wants to help with the bakery."

Tessa blinks, surprised. "Wait, what? Help how?"

I bite my lip, feeling a mix of excitement and hesitation. "He wants to be an investor. Like, a serious one. He said he believes in what we're doing, and he wants to put money into it, help us grow."

Tessa's mouth falls open slightly, and for a moment, she's quiet, processing. Then she sets her coffee down and leans in, her eyes wide. "Whoa. That's... huge, Ivy. But are we really going to let Asher Mercer be our investor? What if things get weird? What if this thing with you two doesn't work out?"

I nod, understanding her hesitation because I've had the same thoughts myself. "I know. That's what I keep thinking too. But... I also know that the bakery could really use the help. We've been putting everything we have into it, and having someone like Asher backing us could make a huge difference."

Tessa leans back, chewing on her bottom lip, clearly thinking it over. She grabs her mug, bringing it to her lips like she's about to take a sip before pulling it back. "It's definitely tempting. Obviously, he's smart, connected, and it's not like he's going to micromanage us. But are you sure it won't complicate things between you two?"

I shrug, sipping my coffee to stall for time, and then decide to come clean. "Well... it might already be a little complicated."

Tessa narrows her eyes at me, clearly sensing something more. "What do you mean, 'already complicated'? Ivy, what aren't you telling me?"

A blush creeps up my neck, and I fidget with the coffee cup in my hands. "We, uh... we slept together... twice." I hold up my fingers. "Actually, waaaay more than twice but we've spent two nights together."

Tessa's eyes widen, and for a second, she's speechless. Then she bursts into giggles, setting her coffee aside as she turns to face me fully. "Oh my God, Ivy! You didn't tell me that part! And here I thought you were just baking gingerbread and exchanging shy looks."

I laugh, hiding my face in my hands for a moment. "It just... it happened. It wasn't planned or anything. But, Tessa, it was... amazing. Like, beyond anything I could have imagined. And it wasn't just physical, you know? It felt... real."

Tessa's laughter fades into a warm smile, and she nudges me with her shoulder. "I'm happy for you, Ivy. I really am. I've never seen you this... glowy about someone."

I roll my eyes at the word glowy, but I can't deny that I've been feeling exactly that. "It's still new, though. I don't want to get ahead of myself. But about the bakery—do we take his offer?"

Tessa taps her chin thoughtfully. "I say we weigh the pros and cons. Pro: we'd have some serious financial backing. Con: we'd be tied to Asher's involvement, and if things with you two went sideways, it could get awkward. Pro: his connections could open doors for us we wouldn't have otherwise. Con: it might feel like we're giving up control."

We talk it through for a few more hours, going back and forth until the pros start to outweigh the cons. Tessa leans back, sighing. "You know, as long as we stay clear on our vision and Asher respects that, it could work."

I nod in agreement, feeling more confident. "I think you're right. He's not the type to take over. He trusts us to know what we're doing. I don't think he has any interest in that. He just sees what we have and wants us to truly succeed, and if we sink all of our cash into a down payment, it really handcuffs us."

Tessa grins. "Okay, then. Let's do it."

"Yeah?" I ask, excitement bubbling up. "We're really doing this?"

"We're doing it," she says, holding out her hand for a high five. I laugh and slap her hand, feeling the weight of the decision lift off my shoulders.

Just as we're about to settle back into discussing the next steps, I narrow my eyes at her. "By the way, what was up with you at the holiday party? You were so evasive, pushing me toward Asher all night."

Tessa flushes, her cheeks turning a shade of pink that's impossible to miss. "I wasn't... evasive," she mumbles, looking everywhere but at me.

"Oh, really?" I press, raising an eyebrow. "Come on, Tessa. I know you. What were you up to?"

She hesitates for a moment, clearly debating whether to spill. But then she sighs, giving in. "Fine. It's... Zane."

I blink, caught off guard. "Zane? Asher's brother, Zane?"

Tessa rolls her eyes dramatically. "Yes. He's so... ugh. Annoying. Rude. But also—" She stops herself, her cheeks flushing even more.

I stifle a grin. "But also what?"

"He's... infuriatingly attractive," she admits, exasperated. "And I don't know, there's just something about him that drives me crazy. In both the good and bad ways."

I burst out laughing, leaning over and nudging her playfully. "Oh my God, Tessa! You have a crush on Zane?"

She groans, covering her face. "I wouldn't call it a crush. It's more like... I don't know, he gets under my skin. But in a way that makes me want to... punch him and then kiss him. Maybe have some really hot, bed-breaking hate sex."

I can't stop laughing, and she swats at me. "It's not funny! He's impossible, and yet..."

"And yet you like him," I finish for her, grinning.

She throws her hands up in defeat. "Fine. Yes. Maybe I like him. A little. But he's so infuriating!" she says again, as if that's the only word that can truly capture her feelings. "Why does it have to be him?"

I pat her knee sympathetically. "Well, I think you should go for it. Who knows? Maybe there's more to him than you think."

Tessa groans again, but I can see the tiny smile she's trying to hide. "He's not my type at all."

"No, what you mean is he isn't falling over himself to be with you and you're not used to that," I tease her.

"Or maybe *that's* precisely the draw. My brain just wants him because I know it can't ever be anything. He's too much trouble for me," she says emphatically, as if she's decided she wants nothing to do with him now. Then she giggles again. "Okay, fine. I'll think about it."

After a few more minutes of playful teasing, we get back to business, agreeing to let Asher be part of the bakery plans. With our decision made, we make the calls—first to our lender, then to Suzette, the real estate agent. Each conversation feels like another step forward, and by the time we hang up, I feel a sense of relief.

Tessa grins at me, holding up her coffee cup in a toast. "Here's to new beginnings."

I clink my cup against hers, smiling as I think about everything that's unfolding. "To new beginnings. And maybe a little Christmas magic for you too."

CHAPTER 10
ASHER

I lean back in my chair, watching the skyline of the city stretch out in front of me. The view from my office is something most people would kill for, but today, I'm distracted by something else—someone else, to be more precise. Ivy.

Ever since we talked about the possibility of me becoming an investor in her bakery, I haven't been able to stop thinking about her. Not just about the business aspect, though that's definitely part of it. The idea of helping Ivy and Tessa bring their dream to life excites me. But it's more than that. Ivy has a way of sneaking into my thoughts in ways that have nothing to do with work. The way she laughed the last time we were together, the way her lips felt against mine... Hell, the way she makes me feel like I'm not just Asher Mercer, CEO, but someone real, someone who could be more.

I glance at my phone, a message from Keri sitting on the screen.

KERI

Ivy Calloway is here to see you.

I can't help but smile. I've been hoping she'd come by. My fingers move quickly across the screen.

ME

Send her in.

The anticipation makes my pulse quicken as I stand up and adjust my jacket, trying to play it cool. A few moments later, the door to my office opens, and Ivy steps inside. She looks as beautiful as ever, her brown hair loose over her shoulders, her eyes bright but conveying a hint of nerves. She's holding a folder, but all I can think about is how much I want to pull her into my arms.

"Ivy," I say, crossing the room toward her, "it's good to see you."

She smiles, but there's a nervous energy to her that I recognize immediately. "Hey," she says, holding the folder out as if it's a barrier between us. "I, uh... I wanted to talk to you about the investment."

I take the folder from her hands, setting it down on my desk without even glancing at it. My eyes never leave hers as I step closer, reaching out to brush a stray strand of hair behind her ear. "Business first, huh?"

She blushes, her lips parting slightly as she looks up at me. "That's why I'm here," she says, her voice soft.

I grin, leaning in just enough to close the distance between us. "Is it?"

Her breath hitches, and I can see the way her eyes dart to my lips before she catches herself. She's nervous, I know, but I also know she feels this pull between us just as much as I do.

"Asher," she says, her voice shaky, "we should talk about the investment. I mean, that's why I came here..."

I let her words hang in the air for a moment before I close the gap between us, pressing my lips to hers in a soft, teasing kiss. Her response is immediate, her hands coming up to rest against my chest as she kisses me back, but there's a hesitation there—a nervousness that I don't want to ignore.

When I pull back, her eyes are wide, her cheeks flushed. "Ivy," I say quietly, "you know this is more than just business, right?"

She nods, biting her lip as she looks up at me. "That's what I'm afraid of."

"So," I say slowly, stepping back slightly to give her some space. "You're worried that mixing business and... whatever this is will make things complicated?"

She nods, still not meeting my eyes. "Yeah. Honestly, we haven't even defined what 'this' is, and now we're talking about going into business together. And I know I said I didn't need to define it, that I was happy to just see where it takes us, but I'm worried. It's a lot."

I uncross my arms, pushing off the desk and stepping closer to her again. I reach out, tilting her chin up so she has to look at me. "Okay," I say softly, "then let's define it."

Her eyes widen, and I can see the way her pulse quickens at the base of her throat. "Define it?"

"Yeah." I give her a small smile, trying to ease the tension. "If it makes you feel better, I'm happy to define it. What do you want this to be, Ivy?"

She hesitates, biting her lip as if she's afraid to say the words out loud. I wait, giving her time, but inside, my heart is pounding. I need to know what she wants, because if she's feeling anything like what I'm feeling, then we're on the same page.

Finally, she speaks, her voice barely more than a whisper. "I want... I want it to be real. I want it to be just you. I don't want to be part of your world, Asher. I just want to be part of you."

Her words hit me like a punch to the chest, and I realize how much I needed to hear them. I close the distance between us again, cupping her face in my hands. "Ivy, I don't care about the world I come from. I only care about you. I want it to be just us too."

Relief washes over her face, and I press my forehead against hers, my thumbs brushing gently over her cheeks. "No more wondering what this is," I murmur, kissing her softly. "It's real, Ivy. It's just us. I'm yours and you're mine."

She kisses me back, and this time, there's no hesitation. No nerves. Just us.

When we finally pull apart, she's smiling, and I can't help but smile back. "Now," I say, stepping back and motioning toward the folder on my desk, "let's talk business. You said you wanted to move forward with the investment?"

Ivy nods, her expression shifting into something more serious as she straightens and looks toward the folder I'd set on my desk earlier. "Yeah," she says, "Tessa and I talked about it, and we both think it's the right move. We want to move forward with the investment."

Her words are confident, but I can see the slight tremor in her hands, the way she's trying to stay composed. This is a big step for her—and for us. I admire how she's balancing the personal with the professional, even if it feels a little delicate.

I pick up the folder, flipping it open and skimming the documents she's laid out. My mind flickers back to how we first started talking about this. I wanted to help, of course, but the more we've talked, the more I've seen the potential in what she and Tessa are building. It's not just about supporting Ivy anymore—though that's a big part of it—it's about building something amazing together. And I'm all in.

"That's great news," I say, setting the folder back down and meeting her eyes. "You two are going to kill it. And you know I'm here to help every step of the way. Whatever you need."

Ivy smiles, her nerves seemingly melting away. "Thank you, Asher. I mean that. This feels... right."

I take a step closer, reaching out to touch her arm. "It is right. You and Tessa have worked hard for this, and now you're about to make it happen. I'm just lucky to be part of it."

Her cheeks flush at my words, but there's a quiet confidence in her now that I love seeing. She's finding her footing, and I'm so damn proud of her.

"Now," I say, keeping my voice light, "since we've got the business side sorted, there's something else I wanted to ask you."

Her eyebrows lift in curiosity. "Oh?"

I hesitate for a second, wondering how to phrase this, but then decide to just go for it. I've never been one to dance around something once I've made up my mind. "There's this event coming up soon. One of those big, fancy galas. It's for charity, but it's... well, it's going to be pretty high-profile. Paparazzi and all that."

She tilts her head slightly, clearly trying to figure out where I'm going with this. "Okay..."

I take another step closer, my hand sliding down her arm to take her hand. "I want you to come with me," I say, my voice soft but certain. "As my date. As my girlfriend."

For a second, Ivy just stares at me, her eyes wide, as if she's not quite sure she heard me right. Then, slowly, a smile spreads across her face, and she lets out a small, breathless laugh. "Your girlfriend?"

I grin, squeezing her hand. "Yeah. That's what I'd like it to be. Official. If that's what you want."

She bites her lip, clearly trying to contain her excitement, but it's impossible to miss the way her eyes light up. "Yes," she says, her voice filled with a mix of happiness and relief, "yes, I want that. I want to be your girlfriend."

Before I can say anything else, she throws her arms around me, and I catch her, laughing as I pull her close. "You're sure?" I ask, brushing my lips against her temple. "It's going to be a big event. Lots of people, lots of eyes on us. I just want to make sure you're comfortable with that."

Ivy leans back slightly, her arms still wrapped around my neck, and she looks up at me with a steady gaze. "I can handle it," she says firmly. "As long as I'm with you, I can handle it."

Her words send a surge of warmth through me, and I lower my head to kiss her, slow and deep, letting the weight of everything we've just said settle between us. When we finally pull apart, I press my forehead against hers, holding her close.

"I can't wait," I murmur, my voice low. "We're going to have an amazing time."

Ivy smiles, her fingers gently trailing down my arm before she steps back, looking more relaxed than she had when she first arrived. "Me too," she says, her eyes sparkling with excitement. "I'm really looking forward to it."

THE NEXT FEW DAYS PASS IN A WHIRLWIND OF MEETINGS, PLANS, AND constant back-and-forth calls. Ivy and Tessa have been hustling nonstop to get everything in place for the bakery, and I've been doing everything I can to help where needed, but mostly I've been trying to give Ivy the space she needs to take the lead. I know how important it is for her to feel like this business is hers, not something she's been handed.

I'm in my office late one afternoon, staring out at the city skyline, when my phone buzzes on the desk. I glance at the screen and smile when I see Ivy's name.

IVY

Guess what?

I lean back in my chair, already feeling the excitement in her message.

ME

Tell me.

A few seconds pass, and then my phone buzzes again.

IVY

We got it! The offer was accepted, and we secured the loan. The bakery is officially happening!

I grin, feeling a surge of pride for her. She and Tessa have been working so hard for this, and now it's finally real.

> **ME**
> I'm so proud of you, Ivy. You two did it!

A few moments later, she responds.

> **IVY**
> I'm so excited! We should celebrate.

I can't help but smile at her enthusiasm.

> **ME**
> Absolutely. How do you want to celebrate?

> **IVY**
> I'd love to show you the building. You know, give you a tour of what's going to be our bakery!

I sit up straighter, already feeling the excitement build. Seeing the place in person would make everything feel even more real.

> **ME**
> I'd love that. When should I come by?

> **IVY**
> How about tonight? Around six?

> **ME**
> It's a date.

I count the minutes until I pull up in front of the building Ivy had mentioned, a modest but charming space in a part of town that's quickly becoming known for its small, trendy shops and local businesses. I can already see the potential in the location, even from the outside. This place is going to be perfect for them.

As I step out of the car, I spot Ivy standing by the entrance, her face lighting up the moment she sees me. She's practically buzzing with excitement.

"Hey," I say, pulling her against me, planting a lingering kiss on her lips, one that leaves us both a touch breathless. "You look like you're ready to burst."

She laughs, stepping back to gesture at the building. "I can't help it. I still can't believe this is actually happening. Do you want to see the inside?"

"I'm dying to," I say, following her as she unlocks the door and pushes it open.

The inside is a blank canvas—bare walls, an open floor plan, and plenty of natural light streaming in through the large windows. It's not much right now, but I can see the vision forming in Ivy's mind as she walks me through the space, pointing out where the display cases will go, where they'll set up the kitchen, and how they're going to design the seating area for customers.

"I can see it already, baby. It's going to be amazing, Ivy."

She turns to me, beaming. "You really think so?"

"I know so," I reply, stepping closer to her. "You've got something special here. I'm just so honored you're letting me be involved."

She smiles, looking up at me with so much warmth that it makes my chest tighten. "Thank you, Asher. For everything."

I lean down, kissing her softly. When we pull apart, I take a deep breath, knowing there's one more thing I want to ask her.

"So," I say, brushing a strand of hair behind her ear, "there's that event I mentioned a while back. It's in a few days, and I was wondering... would you still be up for coming with me? As my girlfriend."

Her eyes widen for a moment, and then her face breaks into a wide grin. "Of course," she says, her voice full of excitement. "I'd love to. Did you think I'd change my mind?"

"Not really but I also understand that this isn't just a night at my place or yours; this is big-time. This is... official. Are you sure you're comfortable with that?"

She nods, her expression confident. "I can handle it. I'll be with you, right?"

I grin, pulling her into my arms. "Yeah, you will be."

And with that, I know everything is falling into place. This thing between us—it's real. And I'm determined to prove that to her not only with this event but for the rest of our lives.

The moment we walk into the grand ballroom at the Mercer building, I feel a surge of excitement ripple through me. The air is thick with the hum of conversation, the sound of gentle laughter, and the soft strains of classical music floating from the live band in the corner. Crystal chandeliers hang overhead, casting a warm, golden glow across the room, making everything and everyone look effortlessly elegant. It's the kind of event people dream about being invited to, and here I am, standing next to Asher as his girlfriend.

I still can't quite believe it. Only a week ago, I'd been nervous about where things were heading between us, and now I'm at this glamorous event by his side, and it feels... surreal. Asher is dressed in a sleek black tux, looking every bit the powerful CEO he is, his hand resting lightly on the small of my back as we step farther into the room. There's something intoxicating and so sexy about being here with him, about being *his*.

"Ready?" he asks, leaning down slightly so I can hear him over the soft buzz of the crowd. His voice is low, comforting, and I can't help but smile up at him, nodding.

"Definitely," I say confidently, swallowing down that ever-present fear that this is all happening way too fast, way too easy, that the other shoe is bound to drop.

He grins, his hand giving my waist a gentle squeeze. "Let's make the rounds. I need to say hello to a few people, but I'll make sure we grab some time for ourselves too, okay?"

"Okay," I say, my heart fluttering at the thought. I know these events are a big deal for him—networking, talking to investors and clients—but I'm just happy to be here. Happy to be with him.

As we move through the crowd, I notice the way people's heads turn when Asher approaches. He's magnetic, and everyone in the room seems to know it. He's immediately swept up in conversations —introductions, firm handshakes, and the occasional well-placed joke that has his companions laughing. I hang back slightly, trying not to feel too much like a fish out of water in this world of polished, high-energy elites.

I remind myself that this is his world, and I need to support him in it. This is what he does. He's the kind of guy who owns rooms like this, who thrives on being the center of attention, and I knew that coming into this. So, when a group of business executives pulls him into another conversation, I let go of his arm with a smile and nod, telling myself it's okay. He'll come back to me. We'll have our moment.

But as the minutes tick by, those moments are few and far between. Every time Asher finishes talking to one group, someone else comes up to him, and I watch as he seamlessly navigates the room, switching from one conversation to another like it's second nature. I get a smile here, a touch of his hand there, but before I can say anything to him, someone else is pulling him away.

I push down the small pang of disappointment in my chest and tell myself to get over it.

This is his night, his world. I'm just here to be by his side, and that's enough.

I take a deep breath and wander toward the bar, grabbing a glass of champagne to busy my hands. The cold fizz of the drink gives me something to focus on as I scan the room, watching Asher as he works the crowd. His charm is undeniable, and I can see why everyone in this room wants a piece of him.

He's genuine. In a world of fake people who only want one thing from him, he's rare.

But as much as I try to stay positive, that small voice in the back of my mind starts to creep in. What am I doing here, really? How do I fit into this world? The women gliding around the room in their designer gowns, perfectly poised, perfectly polished... they all seem so at ease here, while I feel like I'm holding my breath, hoping I don't trip over my own feet.

It's high school all over again.

I sip my champagne, trying to shake the feeling, but then I notice something. A group of women standing not far from me, their gazes flicking toward me, then back to each other as they whisper and laugh quietly. One of them, a striking blonde in a sleek red dress, glances at me again, her lips curling into a smug smirk.

I immediately feel a rush of self-consciousness, the heat rising in my cheeks as I turn away, pretending I didn't notice. But the doubt is already creeping in. They know who I am. They know I'm with Asher. Are they judging me? Do they think I don't belong here? I try to brush it off, but the weight of their stares settles over me like a heavy blanket, smothering the excitement I felt when I first walked in.

I need a minute. Just a minute to pull myself together.

I head toward the restroom, my heart pounding in my chest. Once I'm inside, I lean against the sink, taking deep breaths, trying to calm the swirl of emotions threatening to overwhelm me. It's just nerves, I tell myself. *I knew this wouldn't be easy. I'm doing fine.*

But as I turn on the faucet and splash some cool water on my hands, I hear voices drifting in from the other side of the restroom, two women talking in low, conspiratorial tones. At first, I don't pay attention, but then I catch something that makes my stomach drop.

"Did you see her?" one of the women says, her voice laced with amusement. "I can't believe she's here with Asher. She's not exactly his usual type."

"Right?" the other one replies, laughing softly. "Actually, she's cute, I guess, but... seriously, her? I kissed him at one of these events last year and that man could not get enough of my actual curves."

I look down at my body, my narrow hips and less than ample backside. I at least have a solid B cup going for me but that can't compete with the rest of my body that never caught up. My stomach flips, all those stupid insecurities I thought I'd defeated rushing back.

"And I'm pretty sure you spent the night with him after that fundraiser last spring, right?"

My breath catches in my throat. My hands freeze under the water as their words sink in. They're talking about Asher. About being with him. About kissing him. And one of them spent the night with him?

"Yeah," the first woman says, laughing again. "It's funny, though. He's always with someone new. I wonder how long this one will last."

My heart clenches painfully in my chest, and I turn off the faucet, quickly drying my hands as I try to swallow the lump in my throat. I know it's his past. I know he had a life before me, before us. But hearing it like this, from the mouths of women who have been with him, women who are now standing just a few feet away, laughing about it like it's some kind of joke... it hurts.

I push open the restroom door and slip out into the hallway, the noise of the party feeling distant now as I make my way toward a quieter corner of the building. I find a small alcove, hidden away from the crowd, and lean against the wall, pressing my hands to my face as I try to steady my breathing.

This is what I was afraid of. This feeling of being swallowed up by his world, of not being able to keep up. I told myself I could handle it, but standing here now, hearing those women talk about Asher like I'm just the next one in line... it makes me question everything. Am I just another temporary part of his life? Someone he'll move on from when he gets bored?

I don't know how long I've been standing in one spot, lost in my thoughts, but eventually, I hear footsteps approaching. I look up to see Asher, his expression full of concern as he steps into the alcove.

"There you are," he says softly, his brows furrowed as he takes in my clearly upset state. "I've been looking for you. What's wrong?"

I bite my lip, feeling the sting of tears behind my eyes again. I don't want to make a scene, but the words spill out before I can stop them. "I overheard some women in the restroom talking about you," I say quietly, my voice trembling. "One of them said she spent the night with you after some fundraiser last year, and the other one kissed you. And they were... laughing about it, like I'm just the next one in line."

Asher's eyes widen, his face falling as he realizes what I'm saying. "Ivy, I—"

"I know it's your past," I cut him off, shaking my head. "I know it shouldn't matter. But hearing it like that... it hurt. It made me doubt everything."

He steps closer, his hands reaching for mine. "Ivy, I don't know who those women were, but I promise you, I don't care about anyone from my past. I only care about you. I only want you."

I look up at him, the sincerity in his voice clear, but the doubt is still gnawing at me. "I'm not sure I can do this, Asher. I rushed into things because I wanted to believe I could handle being in your world, but now I'm not so sure. I feel like I'm constantly trying to catch up, and I don't know how to compete with your reputation, with... everything. I thought I was stronger and I know this is my issue, my insecurity, but I just—"

Asher's grip tightens on my hands, and his voice is steady but full of emotion. "You don't have to compete with anything, Ivy. I don't care about what anyone else thinks. I don't care about my reputation or this world. All I want is you. I don't want to lose you."

I swallow hard, tears threatening to spill over as I meet his gaze. He's saying everything I want to hear, but the fear is still there, lurking in the background. "I don't know if I'll ever fit into this life of yours."

Asher's gaze is unwavering, his hands gripping mine like he's afraid I might slip away. "Ivy, listen to me. I know this is overwhelming, and I know it won't always be easy. But I promise you, I will make it all worth it. I don't want you to feel like you don't belong. I'll make sure you know how much you mean to me, how much this means to me."

His words hit me hard, tugging at something deep inside me. I want to believe him, want to believe that we can somehow make this work despite the glaring differences between our worlds. But before I can respond, someone approaches us from behind, calling his name.

"Asher! Sorry to interrupt, but we need you for a moment," a man says, gesturing toward the party. "The investors from London are ready to talk."

Asher grimaces, glancing over his shoulder before turning back to me. "I'm so sorry. I'll be right back, I promise. I just need to handle this, and then we'll finish talking, okay?"

I nod, forcing a small smile, even though my chest feels tight. "It's okay. Go."

He squeezes my hands one last time, his eyes full of regret. "I'll be back soon. I promise." And then he's gone, disappearing into the crowd before I can say anything else.

I watch him go, feeling the weight of the conversation settle over me like a heavy cloud. I know he didn't want to leave, and I know his world is full of these obligations, but it still stings. I lean against the wall, feeling drained, my earlier excitement from being here as his girlfriend now dulled by doubt and uncertainty.

As I take a deep breath, trying to steady myself, I hear footsteps approaching. I glance up to see Zane, Asher's older brother, standing next to me. His presence is as imposing as ever, and while his expression isn't unfriendly, there's something in his eyes that tells me this isn't just a casual chat.

"Hey," Zane says, slipping his hands into the pockets of his suit pants. "I saw you over here, thought I'd come check on you."

I offer a weak smile, trying to hide how rattled I feel. "Hey, Zane. I'm fine. Just... taking a breather."

He nods, but I can tell he's not buying it. I've always heard that Zane could see through people's bullshit, that he has a knack for reading people. In the interviews I've read about him and Asher over the years, Asher always made it a point to give credit to Zane's gut and how it's served them over the years in their continued success. Now with him looking at me, I can't help but wonder if he sees right through me as well. He leans against the wall next to me, crossing his arms as he looks out at the party.

"So," he says casually, "you and my brother, huh?"

I glance over at him, unsure of where this conversation is heading. "Yeah, I guess so."

Zane lets out a low chuckle, his eyes still scanning the room. "I'm all for it, you know. You're good for him. Better than anyone else I've seen him with in a long time."

His words should be comforting, but there's something in his tone that puts me on edge. I frown, turning to face him fully. "But?"

He sighs, glancing down at me with a more serious expression. "But I just want to make sure you know what you're getting into with Asher. He's a good guy, but his life... it's complicated. He's always had a lot of people pulling him in different directions, and sometimes it's hard for him to keep his focus where it should be. On the things that really matter."

I swallow hard, feeling the familiar twist of doubt tighten in my chest. "I know it's not easy. I've already seen that."

Zane's gaze softens, but there's still a warning in his eyes. "Look, I'm not saying he doesn't care about you. I've seen the way he looks at you—it's different. But I've also seen what happens when he gets caught up in all of this." He gestures to the glittering party around us. "And it can be hard for him to find his way back. He's got a lot on his plate, and sometimes the people in his life end up... collateral damage."

The words hit me like a punch to the gut. I glance down at the floor, trying to process what he's saying. "Are you telling me to be careful?"

Zane hesitates for a moment before nodding. "Yeah. I guess I am. Asher's got a good heart, but he's always had this way of getting wrapped up in his reputation, in the image he's built. Just... guard your heart, Ivy. Don't let him pull you in too deep without making sure he's fully in it with you."

I look up at him, a sinking feeling settling in my stomach. "Do you think he's not fully in it?"

Zane runs a hand through his hair, looking conflicted. "I think he is, but this life, this business... it can swallow people whole. Just make sure you're not the one left behind, okay?"

I nod, my throat tight as I try to find the right words. "Thanks, Zane. I appreciate the honesty."

He gives me a small smile, patting my shoulder. "You're strong, Ivy. Don't forget that."

With that, he pushes off the wall and disappears back into the party, leaving me alone with my thoughts. I stand there for a moment, staring at the floor as the weight of everything Zane said settles over me.

I thought I could handle this. I thought I could fit into Asher's world and be a part of it without losing myself. But standing here, hearing those women talk about him like he's just another conquest, hearing Zane's warning... it all makes me wonder if I rushed into this too fast. If maybe I wasn't ready for everything that comes with being with someone like Asher Mercer.

I need to get out of here.

Without another thought, I slip out of the alcove and make my way through the ballroom, avoiding eye contact with anyone as I head for the exit. The noise of the party fades behind me as I step outside into the crisp night air, my heart heavy with doubt.

I don't know if I can do this. I don't know if I can be part of his world without getting swallowed up by it.

And the worst part is, I'm not sure if Asher can stop it from happening either.

CHAPTER 12

ASHER

The party becomes a blur after Ivy walks out, her words looping through my mind like a broken record. I force a smile, shake hands, thank people for coming—going through the motions while my thoughts remain elsewhere, circling around the one person who's no longer here. I barely remember saying goodbye to the last of the guests, their cheerful wishes for the holiday season falling flat in my ears. Even the quiet ride back to my penthouse, the sound of the city muffled by the falling snow, is a haze.

But by the time I'm alone in my office, the weight of everything hits me like a punch to the gut. I slump against the edge of my desk, staring out at the Chicago skyline. The city is a sea of glittering lights, the streets below dusted with fresh snow, twinkling like a scene from a holiday card. Normally, this view gives me a sense of accomplishment, of pride. Tonight, it feels cold, hollow.

Because all I can think about is Ivy—about the way her voice cracked when she told me she didn't belong in my world. About the pain in her eyes when she looked at me, like she was bracing herself for a disappointment she'd already accepted.

I press my palms against the cool surface of the desk, trying to steady my breathing, but the memory of her expression tightens around my chest like a vise. I can't shake the image of her walking out, her shoulders tense, as if she was holding herself together by sheer willpower. And I can't stop hearing her voice, brittle and uncertain, as she said, "I just don't think I fit into your life, Asher."

Zane's words echo in my mind, warnings I brushed off too easily before. *She's not like the women you usually date. She's got a future, a vision. Don't mess with that.*

He was right, damn him. I've been so focused on keeping up the image, on maintaining the persona that everyone expects from me—the smooth-talking CEO, the guy who always has it together—that I forgot what really matters. And what matters is Ivy.

She's the first person who's made me feel like I could be more than just the face of a company, more than a carefully crafted image. She's the first person who's seen through the act, who's looked past the charm and found something worth saving beneath it all. And now she thinks she doesn't belong in my life, that she's not enough for me, when all I've ever wanted is to find a way to fit into hers.

I let out a shaky breath, running a hand through my hair as the truth settles like a stone in my chest. I'm not afraid of losing my reputation or my carefully constructed persona. I'm afraid of losing her.

And suddenly, sitting here in my empty office, surrounded by the trappings of success, it hits me just how much I've been lying to myself. I've built my entire life around a version of myself that I thought people wanted to see, but it's never felt real—not the way it did when I was standing beside Ivy in that Christmas market or when I kissed her under the mistletoe and everything else disappeared.

I don't want to live my life behind a mask anymore. I don't want to lose the one person who makes me feel like I don't have to.

With a new determination burning in my chest, I grab my coat from the back of my chair and head for the door. The late hour doesn't matter, even though it's now after midnight. The empty streets, the snow that falls steadily around me, none of it matters. Because it's Christmas Eve, and if there's one thing I know for sure, it's that I have to see her. I have to make her understand that she's wrong—so damn wrong—about not fitting into my life.

The night air is sharp as I step outside, but I barely feel the cold as I make my way to Ivy's apartment. Snowflakes catch on my coat, melting as soon as they touch my skin, and the city around me feels strangely peaceful, like it's holding its breath. My footsteps crunch against the freshly fallen snow, echoing in the quiet, and I can see my breath fogging the air in front of me.

I think about the dozens of times I've made my way through these streets, always in a rush, always with some goal or meeting or deal on my mind. But tonight, it's different. Tonight, I'm not thinking about the next move or how to close a deal. All I can think about is Ivy—her laugh, the way she crinkles her nose when she's deep in thought, the way she makes me feel like I can be more than just Asher Mercer, CEO.

By the time I reach her building, my heart is pounding in my chest, my breath coming in quick, nervous bursts. I hesitate outside, staring up at the dark windows, the quiet wrapping around the building like a blanket. Doubts creep in, whispering that she might not want to see me, that I might have already lost my chance. But I push them aside, clinging to the one truth that's kept me moving forward tonight: I have to try. Because the thought of letting her walk away without fighting for her is more terrifying than anything else.

I press the buzzer for her apartment, my thumb lingering over the button, and wait. I hold my breath, praying she's still awake. A few moments later, her voice crackles through the intercom, sounding surprised and a little wary.

"Hello?"

"It's me."

"Asher? It's late. What are you doing here?"

I swallow, trying to steady my voice. "I need to talk to you. Can I come up?"

There's a pause, a long, agonizing silence, and I brace myself for the possibility that she might turn me away. But then the door buzzes open, and I push inside, taking the stairs two at a time until I'm standing outside her door, my heart pounding harder than ever.

When she opens the door, she's wearing an oversized sweater, her hair loose around her shoulders, and the sight of her knocks the air right out of my lungs. She looks tired, her face free from makeup, her eyes red-rimmed, a wariness in them that cuts deeper than I expected.

"Asher," she says, her voice hesitant, like she's not sure if this is real or some strange dream, "did you walk here?" She notices the snowy clumps in my hair, the shiver that runs through my body.

I take a deep breath, trying to find the words, but everything I rehearsed on the way here suddenly feels inadequate. So I go with the truth, the raw, unpolished truth that's been clawing at my chest since the moment she walked out of that party.

"I'm sorry, Ivy," I say, my voice rough with emotion. "I'm sorry for making you feel like you don't belong in my life. You have no idea how wrong you are about that. And I don't know if I can make you believe it, but I have to try."

She blinks, clearly taken aback, and she wraps her arms around herself, like she's trying to hold back the uncertainty that flashes across her face. "Asher, I... I don't even know what to say. This is all... it's so much. Maybe we should keep things professional. You have this whole world, this life that I can't be a part of. I'm not—"

"Stop," I cut in, my voice sharper than I intended, but I can't stand to hear her doubt herself again. "Stop saying you don't belong. Because you do. You belong with me, Ivy. And if I have to tear down everything I've built just to prove that to you, I will."

She shakes her head, looking down at the floor, her shoulders trembling. "You don't mean that. You don't know what you're asking for, Asher. I've seen the way people look at you, the way they expect you to be. And I don't want to change you. I don't want you to have to tear anything down to be with me. That's not fair to you."

I step closer, closing the distance between us, desperate to make her understand. "You don't have to change me, Ivy. You already have. You've made me see that I've been hiding behind this... this image for so long, I forgot who I was underneath. But when I'm with you, I feel like I don't have to be that guy anymore. I feel like I can just be me. And I don't want to lose that. I don't want to lose you."

She lifts her gaze to meet mine, and for a moment, I see the cracks in her armor—the fear, the hope, the uncertainty. "Why, Asher?" she whispers, her voice trembling. "Why would you risk everything for this?"

I reach out, taking her hands in mine, feeling the chill of her fingers seep into my skin. "Because you're worth it, Ivy. Because you make me want to be better. And because... I think... I know I'm falling for you. I don't know how else to say it, baby, and I'm sorry if it's too soon or too much, but I love you. I'm so madly in love with you, Ivy."

Her breath catches, and for a second, I think I see something soften in her expression. But then she pulls back, shaking her head, her eyes filling with tears. "You don't know what you're saying. You've built this whole life, this perfect image, and I'm just going to ruin it with my insecurities and my too sensitive feelings."

"Maybe I want it ruined," I say, my voice breaking. "Maybe I want to tear it all down if it means I can have something real. If it means I can have you. We can rebuild our life—together."

She stares at me, her lips parting in a silent gasp, and I see the struggle in her eyes, the way she's fighting to hold on to the walls she's built around herself. But I also see the cracks, the places where hope is starting to seep through.

"I'm scared, Asher," she whispers, her voice barely more than a breath. "I'm scared that you'll wake up one day and realize this was all a mistake. That you'll go back to being the guy everyone else wants you to be, and I'll be the one who's left behind."

I reach out, cupping her face in my hands, forcing her to look at me. "I'm scared too, Ivy. But I'd rather be scared with you than spend another minute pretending I don't care. I'd rather take the risk than spend the rest of my life wondering what could have been."

Her eyes shine with unshed tears, and she bites her lip like she's trying to hold back the words she's too afraid to say. But then she lets out a shaky breath, her shoulders sagging as if a great weight has lifted. "Okay," she says, her voice barely more than a whisper. "Okay. Let's try."

The words are simple, but they feel like the start of something, like the first breath after being underwater for too long. I pull her into my arms, holding her tight as she buries her face in my chest, and for the first time in a long time, I feel like I'm exactly where I'm supposed to be.

And as we stand there, wrapped in each other's arms while the snow falls softly outside, I realize that this—being here with her, holding on to something real—is worth more than anything I've ever built.

The sunlight streaming through my apartment windows is soft and golden, casting a warm glow over the small Christmas tree in the corner. The tree's twinkling white lights and a few carefully wrapped presents beneath it set the perfect festive atmosphere. The scent of fresh coffee mingles with the lingering sweetness of gingerbread, making the morning feel magical and calm.

I'm curled up on the couch next to Asher, his arm draped around my shoulders, pulling me close. My head rests on his chest, and I can hear the steady rhythm of his heartbeat, making me feel more at peace than I have in a long time. It's Christmas morning, but instead of the usual rush of the holiday, it feels like time has slowed down just for us.

"I never thought I'd end up spending Christmas morning like this," I say softly, my voice still drowsy. "It's... nice."

Asher presses a kiss to the top of my head, his lips warm and gentle against my hair. "Yeah. It really is."

I tilt my head back to look up at him, and the sleepy smile on his face makes my heart swell. There's a quiet intimacy in this moment, the kind that makes me feel like I'm exactly where I'm meant to be.

It's strange to think how far we've come in such a short amount of time.

"You know," I begin, biting my lip, "we haven't really talked about how and when we'll tell our families... about us." I'm nervous as I ask, unsure of how he feels about making things official beyond just the two of us.

Asher's smile widens a bit, but his eyes stay warm. "I've been thinking about that, too."

I wait for him to continue, my fingers absentmindedly playing with the fabric of his shirt. "So, when do you think we should tell them?" I ask, trying to sound casual, though my heart is racing a little at the thought.

He doesn't hesitate. "How about today?"

I blink in surprise. "Today? As in... right now?"

"Yeah," he says, his voice full of certainty. "You're going to your family's Christmas lunch, right? What if I come with you? And then tonight, we'll go to my family's Christmas dinner together."

I stare at him, waiting for the punchline, but his expression remains serious. "You mean, meet your family tonight? As in, officially?"

Asher nods, a soft smile tugging at his lips. "Yes. I don't want to spend another Christmas without you, Ivy. I want to be with you for every Christmas, from now on. And technically, you have met my parents before and I've met yours, only this time, we'll be introducing each other as more than *just friends.*"

My heart skips a beat, and for a moment, I'm speechless. The weight of his words sinks in, and I can feel the warmth spreading through my chest. He's not just talking about a casual introduction —he's talking about forever. About us being part of each other's families, not just for today, but for the long haul.

"Asher," I whisper, my voice thick with emotion, "are you sure? That's a big step."

He gently cups my face with one hand, his thumb brushing lightly over my cheek. "I'm sure. You've changed my world in ways I didn't expect, Ivy. I don't want to go back to a life without you. I regret not choosing you sooner."

His words catch me off guard, and I feel my eyes welling with tears. I blink quickly, trying to hold them back. "You really mean that?"

"I do," he says, his voice soft but full of conviction. "You're it for me, Ivy. I want to go to your family's Christmas lunch with you today, and then tonight... I want you by my side at my family's dinner. I want to introduce you to them as my girlfriend, as the person I plan to spend my life with."

I don't know why, but hearing him say it like that—so plainly, so honestly—makes my chest tighten in the best possible way. I've always felt like I didn't quite fit into his world, that maybe we were moving too fast, but right now, none of that matters. What matters is this, and the way he's looking at me like I'm the only thing that's real to him.

"I..." I pause, taking a deep breath, my voice unsteady. "Okay. Let's do it. Let's tell our families together. Oh," I say softly, "and another thing... I love you too."

Asher's smile widens, and before I can say anything else, he leans in and kisses me, his lips soft and hungry against mine. I melt into him, feeling the warmth of his love wrap around me like a blanket. When he pulls back, his eyes are bright with excitement, and finally, I feel like everything is falling into place. I clutch his shirt, tugging him toward me.

Within seconds my hands are tangling in his hair, his tongue finding its way down my neck as I lean back, exposing my breast to him.

"God," he groans, his breath hot against my skin, "the thoughts I have about you..." His words trail off as he pulls at my shirt.

"Tell me," I moan against his lips.

"Better yet"—he flashes that sexy grin—"let me show you."

"Please." It's a whispered plea.

His eyes lock with mine, dark with desire as he draws me closer.

The morning sunlight catches the planes of his face, highlighting the intensity in his expression that makes my breath catch.

"You're so beautiful," he murmurs, his voice rough with restraint. His fingers trace down my spine, leaving a trail of fire in their wake. I arch into his touch, my body responding instinctively to his.

"Asher," I breathe, as his lips find that sensitive spot beneath my ear. My fingers clutch his shoulders, feeling the strong muscles flex beneath my touch. The warmth of his skin against mine sends electricity coursing through my veins.

His mouth traces a burning path down my neck, and I tilt my head back with a soft gasp. "The things you do to me," he growls softly, his breath hot against my skin. "You drive me crazy, Ivy. Like nobody ever has. You are my every fantasy."

I run my fingers through his hair, tugging gently as his kisses become more urgent. The weight of him pressing me into the couch makes my head spin with desire. Every touch, every caress feels amplified by the depth of emotion between us.

"I need you," I whisper against his lips, my heart racing as his hands explore with practiced dedication. He knows exactly how to touch me, how to make me melt for him. The Christmas lights blur into stars behind my closed eyes as sensation overwhelms me. He's hard against me, throbbing. I slide my hand down, between us, wrapping my fingers around him.

"Look at me," he commands softly, and I open my eyes to find him watching me with such raw passion it steals my breath. "I want to see you." His thumb traces my lower lip as he drinks in my expression. "I want to memorize every beautiful sound you make." His fingers are already tugging my clothes from my body, his lips finding mine again as we tear and paw at one another.

I lose myself in his kiss, in the perfect rhythm we create together as he slides into me. There's reverence in the way he touches me, worship in every caress. When we finally break apart, we're both panting, completely lost in each other.

"I love you," he whispers against my skin, and I can feel the words vibrating through his chest. "Every inch of you, every part of your soul."

My response is lost in another passionate kiss as we let the moments fade away around us, consumed by each other. The rest of the world ceases to exist—there is only this moment, only us, only the perfect symphony we create together.

"Holy fuck," Asher groans, sitting up after round three this morning. "I think—you might have broken me that time." He laughs, looking back at me sprawled naked across the couch.

"Can't say I'm sorry," I confess.

"And I wouldn't want you to be." He pulls me up to stand in front of him, looking up at my body with the hunger of a starving predator. "If I thought you could handle me"—his voice rumbles as he slides his hand up between my thighs—"I'd take you again." He cups me gently. "But I'd like to save some for later too."

"Why don't you run home, shower, and change while I get ready here?" I say through broken giggles as he pretends to gently bite my breast. "Then we'll head out to the suburbs."

"Deal," he says, standing up, his cock still mostly rigid, even after our marathon session. He quickly pulls on his clothes, planting a long, wet kiss on my lips that has me wanting to tell him to forget what I said and take me back to bed. "I'll be back in an hour or so."

He bounds out of my apartment like a kid on Christmas morning, which is ironic because that's actually what I feel like right now. I dance into the bathroom, blaring Christmas tunes and singing along through my shower.

As I finish getting ready in my bedroom a little later, my phone buzzes with a text alert.

ZANE

Hey, it's Zane. I know this is short notice and it's Christmas morning so no worries if you can't make it, but any chance you could meet for a quick chat? I'm in your neighborhood.

I chew my bottom lip nervously, glancing at the time. In my excitement, I got ready in almost record time, leaving me enough time to meet with him. I type out a quick response, hitting send and grabbing my coat to head downstairs.

ME

Sure thing. Meet me at the coffee shop on the corner of 114th in five.

Zane is already there when I arrive, two cups of coffee waiting on the table. His expression is serious as I slide into the seat across from him.

"You really were in my neighborhood." I laugh nervously.

"I was outside your building actually," he says, pushing one of the cups toward me.

"Thanks." I gesture with a nod toward the coffee. "Outside my building?" I crook a brow. "And how'd you get my number by the way?"

"Uh..." His eyes shift from mine with a nervous laugh. "I took it from your file. I could have asked Asher for it, same with your address, but I had hoped"—he lifts his gaze up to meet mine again—"that we could keep this between us?" I don't respond, letting his pause linger for a few uncomfortable seconds. "I have to be honest, I wasn't sure you'd come."

"Because of our last conversation?" I ask, wrapping my cold hands around the warm cup. "When you warned me about Asher?" I don't mean for it to sound passive aggressive but there's a sting to my words.

He winces slightly. "Look, Ivy, about that... I know it probably seemed out of line, and maybe it was, but I'm not sorry I said it. That's not what this is about." His gruff tone is back. "I need to know if you're serious about him. Because he's serious about you—more than I've ever seen him with anyone."

"I am," I say firmly. "I know you were trying to protect me when you told me to be careful with him, but Zane, I think I understand him better than you realize."

He studies me for a moment, a strange mix of emotions crossing his face. "You know, it's funny how life works out sometimes. The right people have a way of finding each other, even if the timing isn't what you'd expect."

"What do you mean?"

He takes a sip of his coffee, seeming to choose his words carefully. "Let's just say I've watched Asher go through relationships that were never quite right. Always something missing, always... settling. But with you—" He pauses, a knowing look in his eyes. "It's like watching someone finally find what they've been looking for all along."

"It's not just him," I admit softly. "I've never felt this way about anyone before."

"I can tell." He leans back in his chair, his expression softening. "It's not just you I was trying to protect," he admits, running a hand through his hair—a gesture so similar to Asher's it makes me smile. "After seeing him stupidly fall head over ass for different women over the years, thinking they actually loved him and not his money..." He shakes his head. "I couldn't bear to see him get hurt again. But the way he looks at you..." He pauses, a small smile finally breaking through his serious demeanor. "Actually, I've only seen him look like that back in the day, before all of this actually..." He gestures with his hand aimlessly.

My curiosity piques. "Oh?"

He just shakes his head, that knowing smile still playing on his lips. "That's his story to tell. But let's just say some things are worth waiting for."

"I love him," I say simply, surprising myself with how easily the words come.

Zane's smile widens. "I know. That's why I wanted to see you before you headed out today. I wanted to apologize for being so...

protective before. And to tell you that I'm glad it's you. You're exactly what he needs—what he's always needed."

I feel my eyes getting misty at the weight of his words, sensing there's more meaning behind them than I fully understand. "Thank you, Zane. That means a lot."

He reaches across the table and squeezes my hand. "Just promise me one thing?"

"What's that?"

"Make him happy. He deserves it. You both do." He pauses, then adds with a gentler tone, "And Ivy? Don't you fucking dare tell Tessa I have a heart." And with that, he tosses me a wink. "Merry Christmas." Then he walks out.

By the time I get back to my apartment, Asher has sent me a message that he's on his way back.

"How'd you get here so fast?" I laugh, swinging open my front door. He's bent over, his hands on his knees as he pants, his hair still damp from the shower.

"Because I didn't want to be away from you for another second." He pulls me into a kiss, and I can't help but smile against his lips, thinking about Zane's words. I can't shake the feeling that he knows something I don't, like he's watching the final pieces of a puzzle fall into place.

THE DAY FLIES BY IN A BLUR OF EXCITEMENT. AFTER SPENDING THE QUIET morning together, we finally get ready to face what's next: introducing Asher to my family as not just a guy I went to high school with. As we pull up to my parents' house for lunch, I can feel the nervous energy buzzing under my skin. It's not that I don't think they'll like him—of course, they will—but telling them that I'm head over heels in love with a man I've only reconnected with a few short weeks ago after never really talking in high school... will be a bit of a shock.

Asher squeezes my hand as we walk up to the front door, his presence calming me just enough to keep my nerves at bay. "You ready?" he asks, his voice full of warmth.

I nod, squeezing his hand in return. "Ready."

The door opens, and we're immediately met with the familiar chaos of a family Christmas—laughter, the smell of food, and the sound of my mom calling out from the kitchen. My mom greets us first, her eyes widening in surprise when she sees Asher standing beside me.

"Well, look who's here!" she exclaims, pulling me into a hug before turning to Asher. "And who's this handsome man?"

I glance up at him, feeling a rush of warmth. "Mom, this is Asher Mercer." Her brow furrows in confusion. "From high school."

"Oh my goodness!" she exclaims, recognition coming into her eyes. "Oh my, you have certainly grown up. You are so handsome." She gushes, making my cheeks flush in embarrassment.

"And he's my... boyfriend."

There's a moment of silence as the word settles in, and I feel Asher's hand tighten in mine. But then my mom breaks into a wide smile, immediately pulling him into a hug. "Well, it's about time we met the man who's been making our Ivy smile! Gary, come meet Ivy's boyfriend; I told you; I knew it was a man that got our girl all wound up!" She looks at me, and adds, "I told your dad you must have met a man. I knew something was different about you lately."

The ice is broken, and soon enough, Asher is introduced to the rest of my family. The conversation flows easily, and the tension I felt earlier slowly melts away. My dad and brothers seem to like him, and my mom is already chatting with him as if he's been a part of the family for years.

Through it all, Asher never lets go of my hand, his presence a constant reminder that we're in this together. And as the afternoon unfolds, I start to believe it—that maybe we really can make this work. The only thing still making doubt creep in is the dinner tonight at his parents' house.

Asher's hand rests on my knee, his thumb tracing slow, soothing circles against my skin as we navigate the winding roads toward his family's grand home.

"You're nervous again," he says, glancing over at me with a small smile.

I laugh softly, nodding. "Of course I'm nervous. This is a big deal."

He reaches over, taking my hand in his and bringing it to his lips for a quick kiss. "They're going to love you, Ivy. You don't have to worry about a thing."

I smile at him, but the nerves are still there, bubbling just beneath the surface. Meeting Asher's family feels different from introducing him to my own. There's a weight to it—a significance that I can't ignore. Asher's world has always felt larger than life, filled with expectations and a spotlight that I've never quite been comfortable under. But being here with him, knowing he wants me by my side, gives me the courage to face whatever comes next.

As we pull into the long driveway leading up to the Mercer estate, the grand house looms ahead, festively lit with twinkling lights that reflect off the snow-covered lawn. The place is breathtaking, but it only makes my heart race faster. Asher must sense my nerves because he squeezes my hand again, his reassuring smile never wavering.

When we step inside, the warmth of the house immediately wraps around us, and I'm greeted by the sounds of laughter and the clinking of glasses. His family is gathered in the large living room, and the atmosphere is surprisingly cozy, considering the size and grandeur of the estate. It feels like a home—not the intimidating place I'd built up in my mind.

"Asher!" a voice calls out from across the room, and soon a tall woman with striking features approaches us, her eyes twinkling with amusement as she hugs him tightly. She looks familiar, not just because she's related to Asher but because she was a few years younger than me in school and I remember seeing her in the hallways. "It's about time you showed up."

Asher chuckles and returns the hug before turning to me. "Ivy, this is my sister, Claire."

Claire's eyes soften as she takes my hand, her smile warm and genuine. "So, you're the one we've heard so much about. It's great to finally meet you."

I blush, but her easygoing demeanor quickly puts me at ease. "It's great to meet you too."

"Oh, Asher, sweetheart." His mother rounds the corner, then freezes, a megawatt smile that matches Asher's spreading across her face. "Ivy Calloway?" Her eyes grow wide. "Oh my goodness, you're just as striking as you were in school." She reaches her hands out toward me and I'm shocked she remembers me.

"Hi, Mrs. Mercer, It's so nice to—"

"It's Annabelle," she cuts me off, her eyes already full of tears as she pulls me in for a hug so tight it almost squeezes the air out of my lungs. "I'm so happy he found you again," she whispers softly in my ear.

I make a mental note to ask Asher what she means later, when we are alone.

"Now, let's go introduce you to everyone," she says, her hand in mine as she tugs me toward the kitchen.

The rest of the introductions follow seamlessly—aunts, uncles, and a few cousins, all welcoming me into their world with open arms. The Mercer family is charming and down-to-earth, and despite my initial anxiety, I find myself relaxing. By the time we sit down for dinner, I feel like I'm not just meeting Asher's family, but becoming a part of it.

Throughout the evening, Asher stays close, always checking on me, his hand brushing mine under the table or his arm draped over my shoulders. Every touch, every glance reminds me that this—us—isn't temporary. It's something real, something lasting.

As dinner winds down and the plates are cleared, the conversation shifts to lighthearted stories, laughter filling the room. I find myself laughing along, enjoying the banter and the playful teasing that comes with being in a family that knows each other so well.

At one point, Asher's father raises his glass for a toast, and as everyone lifts their glasses, Asher turns to me with that same loving, intense gaze that always manages to steal my breath away.

"Merry Christmas, Ivy," he whispers, clinking his glass against mine.

I smile up at him, my heart swelling with affection. "Merry Christmas, Asher."

The warmth between us is palpable, and as the evening continues, I can't help but think about how much my life has changed in such a short amount of time. This Christmas has been unlike any other, not just because of the festivities or the gatherings, but because of him—because of the way he's woven himself into my life so completely, so unexpectedly.

As the night winds down and people begin to say their goodbyes, I realize something I hadn't fully grasped before: I'm not just a guest in Asher's life—I'm a part of it now. And he's a part of mine.

When we finally step outside into the cold night air, Asher pulls me close, his arm wrapped around my shoulders as we walk back to the car.

"How are you feeling?" he asks softly, his breath visible in the crisp air.

I smile, leaning into him. "I feel... happy. Really happy."

He presses a kiss to the top of my head. "I'm glad. This is just the beginning, you know. Us, our families... this is our life now."

I look up at him, the man who has changed everything for me in the most beautiful way possible. "I know," I whisper, my heart full, "and I can't wait for all the Christmases to come."

He smiles down at me, his eyes filled with the same love and promise that I've come to cherish. "Neither can I."

I remember his mother's words from earlier and can't hold back my curiosity any longer.

"Asher?" I say softly as we walk toward the car, our footsteps crunching in the snow. "Can I ask you something?"

He pulls me closer against the cold. "Of course."

"Earlier, when your mom hugged me, she whispered that she was glad you found me again. What did she mean by that?"

Asher slows his pace, and I feel him take a deep breath. In the glow of the Christmas lights, his expression is tender but almost shy—something I rarely see from him. A flash of pink even darkens his cheeks.

"Remember how I said I regretted not choosing you sooner?" He stops walking entirely, turning to face me. "Back in high school, I had the biggest crush on you. I used to talk about you all the time at home—how smart you were in AP Literature, how your laugh would carry down the hallway, how you always helped other students with their work. But I never had the courage to really talk to you then. I was... intimidated, believe it or not."

My mouth falls open slightly. "You were intimidated by me?"

He laughs softly, reaching up to brush a snowflake from my cheek. "You were this bright, beautiful force of nature. Everyone loved you, and I was just... me. I relied on my looks and my status as a football star and Mr. Nice Guy." He rolls his eyes at himself. "My mom used to tell me to just ask you out, but I never did. When we reconnected, she knew exactly who you were the moment I mentioned your name. She's been hoping for this for longer than you know."

I feel tears pricking at my eyes, touched by this revelation. "Why didn't you tell me before?"

"I was waiting for the right moment," he says, pulling me close. "And somehow, standing here in the snow on Christmas night, it feels pretty right."

I bite my lip, thinking about my earlier conversation with Zane. "Did... did Zane know about your crush back then too?"

Asher's laugh rumbles through his chest. "Oh God, yes. He used to tease me mercilessly about it. Every time you walked by in the hallway, he'd elbow me or make these ridiculous faces. He probably knew about it even before I told him—he's always been able to read me like a book."

"That explains some things," I say softly, thinking about Zane's protective nature.

"What do you mean?" Asher asks, curiosity clear in his voice.

I snuggle closer to him, breathing in the crisp winter air. "He's just... really protective of you. He wants the best for you, and he made sure I knew that. I think maybe he remembered how much you cared back then, and he wanted to make sure I understood what this means to you now."

Asher's arms tighten around me, and I feel him press a kiss to my temple. "That sounds like Zane. Always looking out for his little brother." He pauses, then adds softly, "But he doesn't need to worry. What we have... it's everything I dreamed about back then, and so much more than I could have imagined."

He plants a kiss on the tip of my nose. "I should have told you all of this sooner, shouldn't I?"

Warmth spreads all the way down my toes that curl inside my boots. "I dunno." I shrug. "I think this moment turned out to be pretty perfect."

We stand in each other's embrace next to the car for several more seconds. "Well, are you ready to head back to the city? I think it's only fair we spend the final few hours of Christmas with just us since it won't always be this way."

"What do you mean?" I look up at him, my nose scrunched.

"First comes love…" He smiles, stepping back to open the passenger car door for me.

"Oh yeah?" My smile is giddy as he closes the door and walks around to climb into the driver's seat.

"Mm-hmm, and then comes marriage." He says it as if he's explaining something complex, keeping a straight face as he turns the car on.

"And then?" I can't hide the excitement any longer as my belly flips at the thought of what comes next. He reaches his hand over, sliding his fingers through mine.

"Then comes all the delicious, naughty baby-making activities." He bounces his eyebrows, causing me to fall into a fit of giggles. "I can't wait to make you a mom, baby. You're going to be incredible." He pulls my hand to his lips, kissing the back of my palm. "And even more, I can't wait to love you and our babies forever."

As we drive away from the Mercer estate, hand in hand, I know without a doubt that this Christmas—this year—has been the start of something wonderful. Something I'm ready to embrace, every step of the way.

No more doubts. No more what-ifs. Just me, Asher, and his promise to always love me.

EPILOGUE
ASHER

The soft glow of the dimmed lights in my apartment reflects off the windows, casting a warm, intimate ambiance over the room. The quiet hum of laughter and conversation drifts through the air as a few of my closest friends mingle with drinks in hand, waiting for the clock to strike midnight. Ivy is by my side, her hand tucked comfortably into mine, and I can't help but feel like this is exactly where I'm supposed to be.

It's New Year's Eve, and while it's a far cry from the glitzy galas I used to attend in previous years, this small, private gathering in my apartment feels a million times better. It's relaxed, it's intimate, and most importantly, Ivy's here with me.

Tessa is chatting with a few friends by the kitchen island, but her eyes keep flicking over to where Zane is leaning against the far wall, looking bored and smug at the same time. I've noticed the tension between them for a while now, though they act like they can't stand each other. Zane will make some snide remark, Tessa will snap back with equal fire, and they'll pretend like they aren't completely drawn to each other. It's becoming increasingly obvious—at least to Ivy and me—that something's brewing between them.

"You look like you're plotting something," Ivy teases, squeezing my hand. Her eyes sparkle with amusement as she watches me watch Zane and Tessa.

I chuckle, leaning down to whisper in her ear. "Zane and Tessa. They've been dancing around each other for weeks."

Ivy laughs softly, following my gaze as Tessa shoots Zane a look of pure annoyance. He smirks, clearly enjoying getting under her skin.

"Oh, they're definitely into each other," Ivy says, shaking her head. "They just don't know how to admit it yet."

"Or they do, but they'd rather argue about it than face the truth," I reply, my eyes gleaming with amusement as I watch Tessa cross the room, her body language tense with irritation. Zane doesn't seem to mind; in fact, he seems to thrive on getting her all worked up.

Tessa huffs as she approaches him, arms crossed. "Do you always have to make everything a competition, Zane? Can't you go one night without trying to win at something?"

Zane, leaning casually against the wall, smirks in that infuriating way only he can. "Winning's in my nature, Tessa. You're just mad because you can't keep up."

Her eyes narrow, and she steps closer, her chin tilted up in defiance. "I can more than keep up, thank you very much. I just don't feel the need to prove it to everyone every five seconds."

Zane's smirk widens. "You say that like you aren't constantly trying to one-up me."

Ivy nudges me with her elbow, and we exchange a knowing look. "They're hopeless," she whispers, trying not to laugh.

"They're going to tear each other apart before they figure it out," I say, grinning. "Or maybe that's just their version of flirting."

Ivy giggles, shaking her head. "God help them if they ever figure it out."

Zane raises an eyebrow at Tessa, clearly enjoying the verbal sparring. "You know, Tessa, if you spent less time being mad at me and more time having fun, you might actually enjoy yourself for once."

Tessa's lips twitch, but she quickly suppresses the hint of a smile. "I do have fun, Zane. I just don't find your ego nearly as entertaining as you do."

Zane steps closer, his eyes gleaming with a challenge. "Maybe you just haven't seen the right side of me yet."

Tessa blinks, caught off guard by the subtle shift in his tone. She opens her mouth to respond but seems to falter for a moment, her confidence wavering just slightly.

Ivy leans in closer to me, whispering with a grin, "Do you think they'll finally kiss this New Year's or keep pretending to hate each other?"

I smirk, pulling her closer to my side. "They'll probably argue right up until midnight and then pretend like nothing's happening. But I give it a month before they finally crack."

We share a quiet laugh, the buzz of the room fading into the background as the countdown to midnight approaches. I glance around the apartment, taking in the scene of our friends and family gathered together, and for a brief moment, I let myself reflect on how much has changed.

This year started with so many questions, so much uncertainty. I didn't know where my life was headed, didn't know if I'd ever find something—someone—that made me feel grounded, whole. But now, standing here with Ivy, my hand in hers, I know without a doubt that everything has changed for the better.

The chatter in the room starts to die down as someone turns up the volume on the TV, and the countdown begins. Everyone gathers closer, champagne glasses raised, ready to toast the new year. Zane and Tessa are still bickering in the background, though I notice they've inched a little closer to each other.

"Ten... nine... eight..."

The room buzzes with excitement, and I turn to Ivy, my heart swelling with anticipation.

"Seven... six... five..."

I take her hand and gently turn her to face me. Her eyes meet mine, and there's something so pure and full of love in her gaze that it makes my chest tighten.

"Four... three... two..."

I lean in, my lips brushing against hers just as the crowd shouts, "One! Happy New Year!"

The moment the words leave everyone's lips, I kiss her—soft and slow, savoring the sweetness of her, the warmth that spreads between us. She melts into me, her arms wrapping around my neck as the rest of the room fades away. It's just us, wrapped in this perfect moment.

When we finally pull away, I rest my forehead against hers, my hands gently cupping her face. "You've changed my world, Ivy. You've made me realize what's important, what it means to really live. I can't wait to spend the rest of our lives together, making more memories like this."

Her eyes shine with tears, but her smile is radiant. "I love you, Asher," she whispers, her voice shaky. "You've changed my life, too. I never thought I'd find something this real, this... perfect."

I kiss her again, my heart full to bursting. "Here's to us," I murmur, our lips still inches apart. "And here's to the best year yet."

We toast with our champagne glasses, the rest of the room cheering and celebrating around us, but nothing else matters except for the woman standing in front of me. Ivy is my world now, and I can't wait to spend forever with her.

Want a sneak peek of Tessa and Zane's story in *Stuffed*? Keep reading for a delicious morsel of book 2 in the Sugar & Spice duet.

STUFFED

Sugar
& Spice

ALEXIS WINTER

PROLOGUE
IVY

I sit cross-legged on Ivy's apartment floor, surrounded by rejection letters from banks. The late afternoon sun casts long shadows across the scattered papers. I pick up the most recent one, from Chicago First National, and read the familiar words again: "While your business plan shows promise..."

"Stop torturing yourself," Ivy says, grabbing the letter and crumpling it. "We knew traditional funding would be a long shot."

"Seven banks." I pull out my meticulous spreadsheet. "Seven rejections. Maybe we're crazy to think we can do this."

"Not crazy." Ivy opens her laptop, showing our savings tracker. "Look - my catering side gigs brought in another $2,000 this month. And our online bakery orders are steadily increasing."

I glance at my own numbers - the overtime at my accounting job, the weekend wedding cake orders, the consultation fees from helping other small businesses with their books. Every penny carefully tracked and saved.

"Fifty-eight thousand," I say softly. "We're still forty-two thousand short of what we need."

"But closer than we were six months ago." Ivy pulls out our

vision board - photos of our dream bakery space, sketches of interior designs, magazine clippings of the kind of community hub we want to create.

"Remember why we're doing this," she continues. "Not just for us. For everyone who needs a place to belong."

I think of the homeless teenager I met last week, who I'd bought breakfast for. How his eyes lit up at the simple kindness of warm food. I think of our plans to partner with local shelters, to offer job training and second chances.

My phone buzzes - another wedding cake inquiry. Next to it, a notification from my investment app showing the small returns on our careful savings.

"We're doing this the hard way because it's worth doing right," I say finally. "No cutting corners, no compromising our vision."

"Exactly." Ivy starts pinning our latest profit projections next to the vision board. "And when Asher Mercer sees our presentation tomorrow..."

"He'll see we're not just dreamers." I straighten my shoulders. "We're fighters."

The sun sets as we work, updating spreadsheets and refining projections. On my phone, another notification pops up - this time from my parents' RV blog, showing them at the Grand Canyon. I ignore it, focusing instead on our growing savings total and not on the fact that sometimes, I selfishly wish my parent's had a huge secret savings account squirreled away for me. But I know that's not the case and I remind myself that I'll appreciate it more knowing Ivy and I did this on our own.

Because some dreams are worth the struggle. And some fighters are worth betting on...Even if we have to bet on ourselves first.

CHAPTER 1

TESSA

The Mercer holiday party is exactly what you'd expect from two brothers who've built an empire—glitzy, glamorous, and overflowing with champagne. The penthouse sprawls across the entire top floor of their downtown building, its floor-to-ceiling windows offering a panoramic view of the city skyline and a very coveted, direct view of Lake Michigan.

"Hate to think what this view cost," an older woman mutters next to me.

"Yeah," I reply politely with a nervous laugh, about to introduce myself since I am here to mingle but she turns and walks away about as quickly as she appeared. I turn around to face the room—large crystal chandeliers cast a warm glow over the space, which is decked out in twinkling lights and garlands, and a giant Christmas tree that almost touches the vaulted ceiling. The ornaments alone probably cost more than my monthly rent. In fact, I'm almost positive I saw a Tiffany's label hanging off of one of them.

The room is beautiful, and I should be soaking in the scene, networking with the city's elite who are scattered throughout the room, but my mind's too busy racing with secret little thoughts about...*him.*

I scan the room, looking for my best friend Ivy who's off somewhere talking to Asher Mercer about our bakery. And while I should be thinking about business and making connections like I told Ivy I would be, my heart has other plans. Specifically, plans that include tracking down a certain Mercer brother—the other one.

The one who used to make my teenage heart race every time I caught a glimpse of him from across the hallway.

The older, bad boy who still haunts my dreams more than I'd care to admit.

As the captain of the cheer squad, student body president and valedictorian of my graduating class—Zane Mercer and I didn't come close to running in the same circles. Apart from the fact he was three years older than me and I was friends with his younger brother Asher, he was also not the kind of influence any young girl's parents wanted their daughter around.

A memory of the last time I remember seeing him in person flashes through my mind. It was the summer after my freshman year of college and I was back in my small town in the suburbs of Chicago. My mom had sent me a text, before I left my apartment in the city that I shared with Ivy, to let me know she saw the Mercer boys in town. She informed me in case I wanted to make a point to say hi to Asher while I was home. I did want to make a point to say hi to *one* of the Mercer brothers...but it wasn't Asher.

The sun was burns the skin of my bare arms as I lift my arm to shield my eyes from it's piercing rays. The summer is starting off strong with temperatures in the high eighties and humidity already nearing August levels. The outfit I took a painstaking amount of time choosing now suddenly feeling too childish when I look down at the flowery, one piece romper that makes me look like an overgrown toddler.

"Shit," I mutter, tugging at the material in an attempt to pull it down a little lower, showing off what little cleavage I have. I straighten my back,

squaring my shoulders as I fluff up my hair and close my car door with my hip.

I may or may not have purposely parked my car on the Main Street in town, right down the block from Mr. Mercer's insurance office, when I noticed Zane's telltale black corvette he's driven since high school.

"You're not an innocent sixteen year old anymore," I whisper to my nearly nineteen year old self, convinced that having finally lost my v-card to a guy in college meant that I was a grown ass woman.

That is until a minute later when Zane himself walks out of his dad's office with his arm around a woman with a body like an actual Coke bottle. For the first time, I understand what that reference meant. His hands move from her waist to her ass, both of them grabbing a handful of her and tugging her closer till she falls against him with a squeal.

I freeze on the sidewalk, my face burning as he backs her against his car, sliding her up onto the hood while he bends her back and drags his tongue down her neck to her tits. It's the middle of the day and Zane Mercer takes the opportunity to once again show the world he doesn't give a fuck about the rules, he's going to do what he wants.

Trying to avoid being noticed, I spin around, tripping over my own feet and falling to one knee. "Ouch!" I wince, glancing down at the red and slightly bloody road rash. But I don't have time to linger, I'm too embarrassed, standing up and limping away back to my car where I cringe silently, praying he was too engrossed in Miss Coke Bottle's tits to witness that.

"You look like you're hunting for someone," Ivy says surprising me. I turn just as she appears beside me with two glasses of champagne. She hands me one, a knowing smirk playing on her crimson-painted lips. Her black dress hugging her body and accentuating her décolletage.

I take a long sip of the bubbles, pushing the embarrassment that still lingers from that memory out of my mind and trying to appear casual even as my eyes continue their covert scan of the room. "I'm networking. Isn't that why we're here?"

"Right," she draws out the word, clearly not buying it. "And your networking has nothing to do with a certain brooding Mercer brother that you secretly swooned over in your diary?"

"I never had a diary," I protest, though we both know that's a lie. "And I have no idea what you're talking about. Besides, shouldn't you be more focused on your own Mercer situation? You should see the way that man has been eye fucking you from across the room."

Ivy blushes, glancing over at where Asher stands talking to a group of investors. Unlike his brother, Asher is all easy smiles and charm, his golden hair catching the light as he laughs at something someone said. "That's... different."

"Different how?" I challenge, but my words trail off as I finally spot him.

Zane Mercer stands by the windows, his back to me, looking just as broad-shouldered and intense as I remember. His dark suit is perfectly tailored, outlining a body that seems even more impressive than it was in high school. His profile is sharp against the glittering city lights as he talks to some suit-clad businessman, his arms crossed, radiating that familiar 'don't approach me' energy that used to both intimidate and intrigue me.

"Go talk to him," Ivy nudges me with her elbow. "You're not in high school anymore, Tess. Now you can use those tits and that ridiculous wit to charm him into bed."

"I didn't say I was going to—" I start to protest, but Ivy's already walking away, throwing me a thumbs-up over her shoulder. I don't know why I feel the need to lie about my intentions with Zane. Sure there's a touch of ego in there, wanting him to see me now that I'm grown up but I'm also not above having a hot, holiday fling with him.

I take a deep breath, smoothing down my red cocktail dress. The one I spent an hour painstakingly choosing just for tonight. The back dips low, leaving my skin exposed, a stark contrast to the high neck. It makes me feel powerful, in control of my sexuality. However, the confidence I've built over the years suddenly feels paper-thin, but I push forward anyway.

The closer I get to him, the quieter the surrounding noise becomes and the louder my stilettos hear clicking against the marble floor. I take in a shaky breath, his back still facing me when I approach him.

"Well, if it isn't Zane Mercer," I say, injecting my voice with more confidence than I feel. "Still avoiding the crowd, I see?"

He turns, and for a moment, something flickers in his dark eyes —recognition, maybe surprise. But then it's gone, replaced by that maddeningly neutral expression he's perfected. His jaw is still as sharp as I remember, his dark hair styled in that purposefully messy way that probably took an hour to achieve. A five o'clock shadow gives his otherwise clean cut image an edge.

"Tessa Marlow," he says, my name rolling off his tongue in that gravelly voice that still makes my stomach flip. "Didn't think you'd be here."

He lifts his glass to his lips, taking a healthy sip. That's when I notice the tattoos on his hands. My eyes must linger on them longer than I realize because his gaze drifts from mine to his own hand with a chuckle.

"No?" I say, pulling my gaze back to his eyes, "And miss a chance to crash a Mercer party?" I raise an eyebrow, channeling every ounce of sass I possess. I pause for a moment, hoping he might reference a memory I still have of seeing him at one of their high school parties. Technically, it wasn't *their* party, it was Zane's party—Asher just let a few of us sneak in. But he doesn't bite so I continue. "Besides, your brother's helping with our bakery. Or didn't you hear?"

His jaw tightens almost imperceptibly. "Heard something about it. Asher's always picking up new..." he pauses, offering a smirk, "projects."

The way he says 'projects' isn't exactly complementary and I don't need to be a genius to see he probably couldn't care less about said project. Ten years later and he still has the ability to get under my skin with just a few words.

"Is that all you think this is? A project?"

163

"Isn't it?" He turns to face me fully now, his height forcing me to tilt my head back to meet his gaze. My mouth goes dry, I forgot what an imposing figure Zane Mercer is. His cologne wraps around me—a scent I'm not familiar with but instantly it makes my head spin. "My brother's always had a soft spot for lost causes."

"Lost causes?" I step closer, irritation making me bold. The champagne probably helps too. "Our bakery is suc—is not a lost cause, Zane. And what a rude thing to say." I lift my glass to my lips to let it go but my frustration gets the best of me. "We didn't come here begging for handouts. We came because your brother saw potential in what we've built. Not that you'd know anything about that, since you're too busy sulking in corners to actually pay attention to what's happening around you."

A ghost of a smile touches his lips, and damn if it doesn't make him even more attractive. "You always did have fire in you, Marlow. Even back in school."

The comment throws me off balance. "You... you noticed me in school?" Instantly I wish I could take it back. My cheeks flush at my moment of vulnerability and suddenly I'm that shy sixteen year old girl all over again.

"Hard not to," he says cryptically, then adds, "You were always around, weren't you? Following Asher like a puppy."

My cheeks burn. "I wasn't following Asher, you jackass. I was—" I catch myself before I can admit I was actually trying to catch glimpses of him. That I used to time my walks to class just so I could pass him in the hallway on the off chance he actually showed up to school.

"You were what?" He prompts, and there's something almost playful in his tone now.

"Nothing," I snap, taking another sip of champagne to hide my flustered state. "God, you're still just as infuriating as you were back then you know that? I thought with age you might have grown out if this.."

"And you're still just as..." he pauses, his eyes trailing over me in a way that makes my skin tingle, "transparent."

"Transparent?" I scoff, even as my heart races. "You don't know the first thing about me, Zane Mercer. You think just because I was the popular cheerleader in high school that you have me..." my words trail off as he takes a step closer to me.

He leans in slightly, and I catch another whiff of his cologne. "No? Then why are you over here talking to me instead of networking with all those potential investors?"

I meet his gaze defiantly. "Maybe I like a challenge."

"Or maybe," he says, his voice dropping lower, "you're still that same girl who used to watch me from behind her little pom-poms, thinking I didn't notice."

My breath catches in my throat. All these years, I thought I'd been so subtle. "I didn't—"

"You did," he cuts me off, a smugness in his tone that both infuri-ates and excites me. "And now here you are, all grown up and still looking at me the same way."

"You're delusional," I manage to say, but my voice comes out breathier than I intended. My plan to have the upper hand on him tonight is quickly dwindling.

He smirks, and the expression is so devastatingly attractive I want to either slap him or kiss him. Maybe both. "Am I? Prove it. Stay away from me for the rest of the night."

It's a challenge, and we both know it. The smart thing would be to walk away, to prove him wrong. To show him that I'm not that same lovesick teenager who used to pine after him. But something keeps me rooted to the spot, my heart pounding as I stare up at him.

"Fine," I say finally, squaring my shoulders. "Challenge accepted. But just so you know, Zane? You're not as irresistible as you think you are."

His laugh is low and knowing, sending shivers down my spine. "We'll see about that, won't we, Marlow?"

I turn and walk away, my heels clicking against the marble floor, feeling his eyes on me the entire time. And despite my words, despite my determination to prove him wrong, I already know I'll be back. Because some things never change—and apparently, my weakness for Zane Mercer is one of them.

As I make my way back to where Ivy stands with Asher, I catch my reflection in one of the windows. My cheeks are flushed, my eyes bright, and I look exactly like what I am—a woman who's just been thoroughly rattled by the man she never quite got over.

God help me.

CHAPTER 2

ZANE

I stalk away from her, my hands shoved in my pockets, trying to ignore the way my body is screaming at me to turn around. To go back. To push her up against that wall and show her exactly what I've been thinking about for the past decade.

But I can't.

She's Tessa Marlow. The girl who used to watch me in the halls with those big doe eyes. The one who made my cock hard in class just by existing. The one who was always too young, too pure, too *everything* for a guy like me.

The halls are dark and quiet, just like they are when I come in early or on the weekends. That's how I like it. Quiet. Uncomplicated. Easy.

"Fuck," I mutter, yanking open the door to my private office and letting it slam behind me. I loosen my tie and pour myself three fingers of scotch, downing half of it in one swallow.

The burn does nothing to erase the image of her in that red dress. The way it hugged every curve, showing off the woman she's become. She's not that teenage girl anymore—she's all grown up and even more tempting than she was back then.

"Shit," I groan, dropping down into my leather chair and closing my eyes, letting my mind wander back to the days when she haunted my every thought.

The numbers blur together as I lean against my Corvette, cigarette dangling from my lips. Another failing business, another stack of reports showing exactly why. Dad might think I'm worthless, but I can read a balance sheet better than half his accountants.

"Just sell the damn thing," I mutter into my phone, watching the snow drift down. "The longer you hold onto it, the more money you'll lose."

The business owner on the other end starts arguing, but I've already stopped listening. Because there she is – Tessa fucking Marlow, pressed against the library window, pretending to study while she watches me.

She thinks I don't notice. They all think that – that I'm too wrapped up in my own bullshit to see the whispers, the stares. But I notice everything. Especially her.

"Listen," I cut the guy off, "my lunch break's over. Call me when you're ready to take my advice."

I hang up, taking a long drag of my cigarette. Through the window, I can see her friend trying to get her attention. Probably talking about the winter formal or some other bullshit I couldn't care less about.

But Tessa's still watching me.

She shouldn't interest me. She's everything I hate about this place – the perfect cheerleader with her perfect life, floating through high school on popularity and pep rallies. The kind of girl who would never look twice at the screwup who got kicked out of four schools.

Except she does look. All the fucking time.

I've caught her staring in the hallways, in the cafeteria, at my brother's stupid parties. Always with those big blue eyes that seem to see right through my carefully constructed walls.

"Fuck this," I mutter, crushing my cigarette under my boot. I need to get out of here, away from the temptation to look back at her.

The bell rings as I'm heading to the parking lot. I round the corner and suddenly she's there, crashing into my chest like some kind of cosmic joke.

"Shit, sorry," I say, my hands moving to steady her before she falls.

She's smaller than I expected, delicate almost, but there's strength in the way she carries herself.

"It's okay," she squeaks, and something in my chest tightens at the sound. "My fault."

I look down at her, and for a moment, I let myself really see her. Not just the cheerleader uniform or the perfect blonde ponytail, but her. The intelligence behind those eyes. The slight tremble in her lower lip. The way her breath catches when I touch her.

It would be so easy to keep holding her. To back her up against the lockers and find out if she tastes as sweet as she looks.

Danger flashes in my mind.

"You're Asher's friend, right?" I force myself to let go, step back. "The cheerleader?"

"Tessa," she says, and fuck if her breathless voice doesn't do things to me. "We've actually met before. At your house, when——"

"Right." I cut her off before she can remind me of that night – her in those tiny shorts, laughing at something my brother said while I watched from the shadows, wanting what I couldn't have. "Tell my brother I need those car keys back by six."

I walk away before I can do something stupid, like ask why she watches me. Like tell her I watch her too.

In my next class, I can't focus on anything except the lingering warmth of her body against mine. The way she fit perfectly in my hands. The soft catch in her breath when she said my name.

This is exactly why I keep my distance. Girls like Tessa Marlow are nothing but trouble. They make you want things you can't have, dream about futures that don't exist for guys like me.

My phone buzzes – another failing business owner wanting advice. Good. Numbers I can handle. Balance sheets don't make promises they can't keep. Profit margins don't look at you with eyes full of possibilities.

But as I stare at the spreadsheet, all I can think about is the way she whispered my name. How her whole body seemed to lean into my touch, like she wanted more.

Like maybe she sees past the bad boy exterior to something worth wanting.

"You're fucked," I mutter to myself, shoving my phone away. Because she's seventeen and innocent and everything I'm not.

Because wanting her is dangerous.

Because for the first time in my life, I'm not sure I'm strong enough to keep my distance.

I light another cigarette, trying to burn away the memory of her body against mine. But it's no use. Tessa Marlow has gotten under my skin, and I'm starting to think she's been there a lot longer than I want to admit.

God help us both.

The memory fades as I stare out my office window, the Chicago skyline a stark contrast to those high school parking lot days. Ten years, and she still has the same effect on me. Still makes me want things I have no business wanting.

The door opens behind me. "You're brooding again."

"I don't brood." I don't turn around. Asher knows me too well – he'll see right through my bullshit.

"Right." He drops into one of my leather chairs. "Just like you weren't just thinking about Tessa Marlow."

Now I do turn, fixing him with a glare. "Don't start."

"Come on, Zane. I saw the way you looked at her tonight. The way you've *always* looked at her."

"I don't look at her any way." I loosen my already loose tie, needing more air. "She's an annoyance."

"She's more than that and you know it." He leans forward, suddenly serious. "You've wanted her since high school."

"Ancient history."

"Is it?" He raises an eyebrow. "Because the tension between you two out there," he shakes his head with a whistle, "could sense it from across the room."

I pour us both a scotch, buying time. "What do you want, Ash?"

He accepts the glass, but his expression stays serious. "I want my brother to be happy for once in his fucking life. To stop punishing himself for things that happened a decade ago."

"I'm fine."

"You're alone." He takes a sip. "And don't give me that bullshit about preferring it that way. We both know that's not true."

I sink into my chair, suddenly exhausted. "What about you and her friend?" I give him a knowing look, "Ivy Calloway."

His face softens at her name, and I know I've successfully diverted his attention. "That obvious, huh?"

"Only to someone who knows you." I study him over my glass. "You're clearly still obsessed."

"Yeah." He runs a hand through his hair – a nervous tell we both inherited from our father. "There's just something about her, you know? She's brilliant and driven, but there's this softness too. This way she has of making everyone around her feel... seen."

"Sounds like true love." My sarcastic tone is obvious, my distrust of her not so much.

"Maybe." He grins. "I'm helping with their bakery, did you know that? The business plan is solid. They've really thought it through."

I think of Tessa's fierce defense of their venture earlier. "Yeah, I got that impression."

"You should see Ivy when she talks about it. Her whole face lights up." He shakes his head, like he just said some super human thing. "I've never met anyone like her."

"Just be careful," I warn. "Mixing business and pleasure—"

"Is exactly what you should be doing with Tessa."

I set my glass down harder than necessary. "We're not talking about me."

"Aren't we?" He leans back, studying me. "You pushed her away back then because she was too young. What's your excuse now?"

"She deserves better than me." The words slip out before I can stop them.

"That's not your decision to make." He stands, draining his glass.

"She's not that teenage girl anymore, Zane. And you're not the same angry kid you were back then."

"Some things don't change."

"But people do." He heads for the door, pausing with his hand on the knob. "You know what I think? I think you're not afraid she deserves better. I think you're afraid she'll actually want you – the real you. And then you'll have to stop hiding behind those walls you've built."

The door clicks shut behind him, leaving me alone with thoughts I've spent years trying to bury. Memories of blonde hair and bright smiles. Of watching her from a distance, wanting what I couldn't have.

But Asher's right – she's not that girl anymore. She's a woman now, successful and confident and sexy as hell. A woman who stood up to me tonight, who pushed back against my walls like they were made of paper.

A woman who still looks at me like she sees something worth wanting.

I reach for the scotch again, but stop myself. Liquid courage isn't what I need right now. What I need is to figure out how to keep my distance when everything in me is screaming to pull her closer.

Because if I'm honest with myself – really honest – I'm not worried she deserves better than me.

I'm terrified she'll realize I'm exactly what she's been looking for all along.

And then what the fuck am I supposed to do with these walls I've built?

I have no idea how long I've been wallowing on my couch once I manage to make it home from the party, but my phone buzzes in my pocket—bringing me back to reality. I'm tempted to ignore it. It's probably Asher, wanting to dissect the party, to talk about investors and deals. But when I pull it out, there's a notification from an unknown number:

UNKNOWN

Just wanted to make sure you got home okay. The snow's getting pretty bad out there. - T

I stare at the message, my thumb hovering over the screen. How the hell did she get my number? Asher, probably. He's always sticking his nose where it doesn't belong.

I should ignore it. That would be the smart thing to do—maintain the distance, keep the walls up. But something makes me type out a response:

ZANE

I'm fine. How did you get this number?

Her reply comes almost immediately.

TESSA

Your brother might have slipped it to me. Don't be mad at him—I can be very persuasive when I want to be.

I can almost hear her voice, that teasing lilt she gets when she's being playful. Despite myself, I feel a smile tugging at the corners of my mouth. I glance at the clock.

ZANE

I'm sure you can be. But that doesn't mean you should be texting me at midnight.

Three dots appear, disappear, appear again. Finally her reply appears.

TESSA

You're right. I'll leave you alone. But just so you know, Ivy and I will be at the the bakery at 7am tomorrow if you're interested in the best cinnamon rolls in the city. No pressure though.

I run a hand over my face, feeling that familiar tug of war inside me. Part of me wants to shut this down now, before it goes any further. But another part—a part I've been ignoring for too long—wants to see where this might lead.

ZANE

I'll think about it.

It's not much, but it's more than I would have given anyone else. And judging by her response—a simple smiley face—she knows it too.

I toss my phone onto the coffee table, leaning back against the couch with a sigh. The snow is falling harder now, blanketing the city in white, making everything look softer, more forgiving. Maybe she's right. Maybe I don't have to keep everyone at a distance.

The thought settles in the back of my mind, stubborn and insistent. For the first time in years, I feel like there might be something worth changing for. And that terrifies me more than anything.

Because letting people in means being vulnerable. It means risking disappointment, heartbreak, loss. All the things I've spent the last decade building walls against. But watching Tessa tonight, seeing the way she moves through life with such openness, such hope... it makes me wonder if maybe I've been doing it wrong all this time.

Maybe the real risk isn't in letting people in. Maybe it's in keeping them out.

I get up, walking back to the window. The city stretches out below me, a maze of lights and shadows, and somewhere out there is a bakery that opens at 7 AM. Somewhere out there is a woman who looks at me and sees something worth saving.

My phone buzzes again, but I don't check it.

Instead, I pour one last drink, raising it to my reflection in the window. "Here's to taking chances," I murmur, and for once, the silence in my apartment doesn't feel so hollow.

Maybe it's the bourbon, or maybe it's just the lingering effect of seeing her again after all these years, but as I head to bed, I feel something I haven't felt in a long time: hope.

And even though part of me is still screaming that this is a mistake, that I should stick to what I know—numbers, deals, safe distances—I can't help but think about tomorrow morning. About cinnamon rolls and coffee and the possibility of something more.

Something real.

You can order this spicy, enemies to lovers Christmas romance by scanning the QR code below or clicking HERE.

And while you're at it, check out my other Christmas romance stories that are sure to warm you up this holiday season!

Dashing Mr. Snow

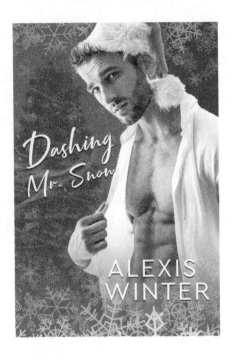

"Maybe we can be a little naughty. You want to be naughty for me, right?"
The last thing I expected to get for Christmas was being dumped by my boyfriend—after all, I'm always on Santa's good list. But walking in on my naked boss and seeing his *candy cane* was an even BIGGER holiday surprise—one that has me headed straight for a lump of coal this year.

Alex Snow, the billionaire CEO of Snow Communications and the only living heir to his family's fortune, has a reputation for being intimidating.

Not in the *"I'm an arrogant bosshole"* kind of way, but more of a "I value my privacy above all else" kind of way.

So imagine his delight when I stumble into what I think is his home office with a contract in hand just as he emerges from the shower.

Only... it isn't his office. It's his bedroom, and the low-slung towel hanging off his hips slides down his muscular thighs, landing in a perfect pile at his ankles.

A Very Bossy Christmas

"Sweetheart, I know exactly how to handle you."
Those eight little words whispered in my ear by my boss were my undoing.
And what we did after he said them, most definitely landed me on Santa's naughty list.
If there's one man who can suck all the joy out of Christmas—it's my boss, Damon Wells.
I should have known when fifteen minutes into our first interview, he told me that nothing about me stood out from the fifty other applicants.
Yet somehow, I'm sitting shotgun in his fancy sports car on the way to my family's house for the week.

Naughty or Nice

ALEXIS WINTER

Dear Santa, I know I'm supposed to be nice, but this year, I need to be really naughty.

Oh, and I need a BIG favor—Carson Wells, in nothing but a big pretty bow under my Christmas tree.

Xoxo, Felicity

A LITTLE BIT ABOUT ALEXIS

Alexis Winter is a contemporary romance author who loves to share her steamy stories with the world. She specializes in billionaires, alpha males and the women they love.

If you love to curl up with a good romance book you will certainly enjoy her work. Whether it's a story about an innocent young woman learning about the world or a sassy and fierce heroine who knows what she wants, you are sure to enjoy the happily ever afters she provides.

When Alexis isn't writing away furiously, you can find her exploring the Rocky Mountains, traveling, enjoying a glass of wine or petting a cat.

Want to follow along with her on social media?
Scan me!

ALSO BY ALEXIS WINTER

Love You Forever Series

The Wrong Brother

Marrying My Best Friend's BFF

Rocking His Fake World

Breaking Up with My Boss

My Accidental Forever

The F It List

The Baby Fling

Dark Romance

No Redemption

Slade Brothers Series

Billionaire's Unexpected Bride

Off Limits Daddy

Baby Secret

Loves me NOT

Best Friend's Sister

Slade Brothers Second Generation

That Feeling

That Look

That Touch

That Kiss

Men of Rocky Mountain Series

Claiming Her Forever

A Second Chance at Forever

Always Be My Forever

Only for Forever

Waiting for Forever

Chicago Billionaire Series

Those Three Words

Just This Once

Dirty Little Secret

Beg For It

Looking For Trouble

Dark as Knight

Very Bad Things

Make Her Mine Series

My Best Friend's Brother

Billionaire With Benefits

My Boss's Sister

My Best Friend's Ex

Best Friend's Baby

Grand Lake Colorado Series

A Complete Small-Town Contemporary Romance Collection

South Side Boys Series

Bad Boy Protector-Book 1

Fake Boyfriend-Book 2

Brother-in-law's Baby-Book 3

Bad Boy's Baby-Book 4

Mountain Ridge Series

Just Friends: Mountain Ridge Book 1

Protect Me: Mountain Ridge Book 2

Baby Shock: Mountain Ridge Book 3

Castille Hotel Series

Hate That I Love You

Business & Pleasure

Baby Mistake

Fake It

**ALL BOOKS CAN BE READ AS STAND-ALONE READS WITHIN THESE SERIES

Made in the USA
Monee, IL
04 December 2024

72279152R00108